A TWO AUTHOR NOVELLA DUET

*must love*

# HIGHLANDERS

TWO SCOTTISH CONTEMPORARY ROMANCES

## GRACE BURROWES

*and*

## PATIENCE GRIFFIN

Published in the two-novella compilation, Must Love Highlanders, by Grace Burrowes Publishing, 21 Summit Avenue, Hagerstown, MD 21740.

ISBN for Must Love Highlanders: 978-1507632260

Cover by Wax Creative, Inc.

# Dunroamin Holiday

GRACE BURROWES

# DEDICATION

Dedicated to my late brother-in-law, Dr. Thomas Edwards Polk, II, PhD. Tom gave me the first sincere compliment I can recall receiving, and since that day (I was about eleven), I've stood a little taller and been a little more confident.

# CHAPTER ONE

"Scottish men are hot, fun, and emotionally unavailable," the travel agent chirped. "Exactly what a girl needs for the perfect vacation."

Louise Cameron hadn't been a girl for years, while the woman madly typing on the other side of the desk—Hi, I'm Cindy!—looked like she'd yet to graduate high school.

"I need peace and quiet," Louise said, "which is why I'll spend my time in a cottage in the Scottish countryside, more or less by myself."

The agent, a perky exponent of the more-highlights-are-better school of cosmetology, swiveled away from her keyboard as a printer purred out an itinerary.

"The Scottish countryside is full of men, braw, bonnie laddies who can hold their whisky, so to speak. Hit the nearest pub and wear dancing shoes. You know the tickets are nonrefundable?"

The question gave Louise a pang. "The charges have already hit my credit card." Jane had insisted as only Jane could, and in a weak moment of rebound impulsivity, Louise had capitulated.

Nonrefundable tickets were cheaper, and a woman who'd

abandoned the lucrative practice of law needed to watch her piggy bank—or return to the practice of law.

"Then you're all set!" Hi-I'm-Cindy! snatched the itinerary from the printer, tucked it into an envelope, and slid the packet across the desk. "Let me know if you have a good time, though I'm sure you will. Scotland is one of the fastest-growing travel destinations on the planet and for good reason. We've had nothing but rave reviews for Dunroamin Cottage, and the scenery is unbelievable, if you know what I mean."

Before Louise could be subjected to a lascivious wink, she stuffed the itinerary and tickets into her purse and rose.

"Thanks, Cindy. I'll tell the braw, kilted laddies you said hello. I'm off to lunch." With the author of Louise's latest misfortune.

Jane had already chosen a table when Louise arrived at their favorite Eritrean restaurant—also the only Eritrean restaurant in Damson Valley.

"Greetings, earthling!" Jane said, bouncing to her feet and kissing Louise's cheek. "If you bailed on your Scottish vacation, I will sue the travel agent."

Jane looked better than ever, her red hair longer than Louise recalled seeing it, her petite figure every bit as perfect. Jane's recent marriage to, and law practice merger with, Dunstan Cromarty was probably responsible for the damned twinkle in her eyes.

"I didn't bail," Louise said. She hadn't bailed *yet*. "What are you working on?"

Lawyer-fashion, Jane had papers spread out on the table. As Louise slid into the booth, Jane gathered up the documents and tucked them into a plain manila folder.

"Big bad divorce proceeding," Jane muttered.

"The best kind." From a billable hours perspective. "Anybody I know?"

Louise flipped open a menu rather than glance at the name on the folder, though as often as she and Jane had eaten here,

Louise could have recited the entrees from the depths of a Chunky Monkey coma.

Jane stashed the paperwork in a shoulder bag that had been known to double as a gym bag, emergency first aid bag, overnight bag, and gourmet goodie bag.

"Nothing's been filed yet," Jane said.

Meaning Louise, because she didn't actively practice with Jane any more, wasn't privy to the details.

"I'm still legally a partner in the firm," Louise said. "Besides, I'm off to Scotland for the next several weeks, and won't have anybody to gossip with."

People underestimated Jane because she was diminutive and pretty. As an attorney, she was also hell in stilettos when she chose to be. That she'd teamed up in every way with Dunstan Cromarty made sense: The big Scot was up to Jane's weight, so to speak.

"Julie Leonard is ditching the handsome buffoon she married in a fit of madness right out of law school," Jane said, squeezing lemon into her water.

"Julie has always been a pleasure to work with." To the extent that a prosecutor could *be* a pleasure to work with when she was trying to put your client behind bars. "Maybe Madam State's Attorney needs a Scottish vacation, too."

Or a Scottish honeymoon. Jane had truly never looked better, for which Louise ought to hate the entire country. Louise pretended to study the menu instead, though her appetite hadn't been spotted since about Christmas.

"Have you heard from Robert?" Jane asked.

*Let the cross-examination begin.* "Yes, I have. He's engaged."

"I'm sorry." Jane's compassion was immediate and sincere, also irritating as hell.

"It's my past all over again," Louise said, putting the menu aside. "I fall for an art professor and he screws me over. The last one stole my glazing process, and this one leaves me with three months on the lease, and for a sophomore whose understanding of art depends on having a mouse in her hand—of one species or another."

"A wee, sleekit, cow'rin, tim'rous beastie, that mouse," Jane smirked. "You're better off without him."

*Brilliant legal deduction.* "Let's order, shall we?"

They had their usual—sambusas, soup, and plenty of warm, vinegary injera bread. Louise ate to avoid a scolding, not because the food appealed.

"Lou, are you okay?"

*Well, hell.* "I will be. The soup is good, don't you think?"

"Louise Mavis Cameron, I am your friend, so stop being polite. If you don't want to teach drawing anymore, then don't. If you don't want to practice law ever again, that's okay, too. A big, wide world will surely offer something you enjoy doing that pays the bills. While you try to figure out what that is, go to Scotland. Dunstan says Wallace will enjoy having some feline company while you're gone."

Louise dipped her spoon in the soup of the day and said nothing. How pathetic was it, that her sole excuse for canceling a very expensive trip abroad came down to the abiding fear that she'd miss her cat?

—◦◦◦◦—

"You should feel sorry for the lass," Jeannie said, turning up the burner under the tea kettle. "She's a lawyer, a spinster, a Yank, and her hobby is throwing pots. Such a blighted soul is surely in need of holidays. She's probably scrimped for years to afford a few weeks in Scotland."

Liam Cromarty felt sorry for *himself*, which unmanly sentiment, Jeannie—a relatively new mother and one of Liam's favorite cousins—would sniff out before the tea kettle had come to a boil.

"Have Uncle Donald show your spinster around then," Liam suggested, plucking an apple from the bowl of fruit on Jeannie's counter. "He's a hopeless flirt, he knows every back road and ruined castle in every shire, and he'll raise her spirits with naughty jokes."

Jeannie took down two mugs, one a bright floral ceramic—Morag's work—the other clear Scandinavian glass. When a baby joined a household, apparently every manifestation of order and organization was imperiled.

"Liam, for shame," Jeannie said, slouching onto a stool at the kitchen counter. "Donald would put the lady in waders and drag her to the nearest trout stream where she'd be pestered crazy by the midgies."

"Donald would also ply the poor dear with good whisky. Sounds like a fine time to me."

The baby on Jeannie's shoulder began to fuss, so Liam plucked him from his mother's grasp.

"Hush, laddie. We'll take you fishing soon enough." The wee fellow peered at Liam from the blue, blue eyes common to Cromarty men of every age. "You must learn to be quiet though, for Donald takes a dim view of a boy who scares away the fishies."

"The little ones always behave for you," Jeannie said, a touch of envy in her tone. "Every bairnie in the family takes to you, no matter how you grouse and brood. You need a holiday too, Liam."

Jeannie was the cousin closest to Liam in age, and more than that, she was his friend. When he'd nearly disappeared into the bottle after Karen's death, Jeannie hadn't given up on him, and for that Liam would always owe her.

He loved her too, and was glad she'd found a man to share her life with.

Truly, he was.

"Can't you ask Morag?" Liam said. "She's the logical choice, being the family potter."

Liam rubbed wee Henry's back, earning a milky-scented baby sigh near his ear. The feel of the child in his arms provoked sentiments ranging from despair to fury to something so tender and vast, he—a man who made his living with words—didn't even try to find a label for it.

"Morag has to build up inventory for this summer," Jeannie said. "She's at her wheel and kiln all the livelong day, and she's not the cheeriest soul."

The kettle whistled, and Jeannie hopped off her stool while Liam continued to rub the boy's back. Morag was a right terror on her bad days. Even when she danced, she brought a ferocity to her grace that Liam understood perhaps better than she'd guess.

The ink was barely dry on Morag's divorce decree. Now was not the time to impose.

"When is this poor refugee from the American legal system to grace Caledonia's shores?"

Liam should not have asked. Jeannie's smile said as much, for the question implied that Liam was rearranging his schedule, making yet another effort to accommodate the vast Cromarty family network. Every auntie, cousin, and in-law assumed a man without wife and children was on call to make up the numbers socially, pitch in on the weekend projects with the menfolk, and otherwise step and fetch on command.

All because they couldn't bear for him to be lonely, of course.

Liam could have told them that activity and family gatherings didn't cure loneliness—something the American spinster probably understood too.

"What does it say about me," he murmured to the child, "that I have something in common with elderly lady lawyers in need of a holiday?"

A wet, unmistakable noise came from the vicinity of the baby's nappy, while Jeannie poured the tea, and Liam made a mental vow to introduce the American spinster to Uncle Donald.

—⁓◌⁓—

The flight from Newark to Edinburgh had been made more bearable by an empty seat to Louise's left, and a little old Scottish lady to her right. Hazel Chapman had once upon a time taken tea with the Queen at one of the Holyroodhouse Palace garden parties, which gatherings were limited to a select few hundred souls whom Her Royal Majesty wanted to honor for civic works.

"I volunteer a lot," Hazel had confided, "because I miss the grandchildren so, but a man must go where there's work, aye?"

Yes, and a woman must too, and that meant another semester teaching drawing, at least. Louise chatted with Hazel through passport control and customs, and as they approached the international arrivals area, endured several invitations to stop by Hazel's wool goods shop in some unpronounceable town in the Highlands.

Hazel referred to her boss as "the laird," and said he lived all by himself in a castle on a loch. Truly, Louise had ended up in Scotland.

They parked their suitcases side by side as Hazel rhapsodized about her whisky fudge recipe—an idea Louise could heartily endorse—but Louise couldn't see anybody holding a sign for "L. Cameron" in the milling crowd.

After making initial arrangements with Jeannie MacDonald, one of Dunstan Cromarty's cousins, Louise had exchanged e-mails with another cousin, Liam Cromarty. She pictured her prospective driver as dour, reliable, and safe. The airport crowd included plenty of sturdy, tweedy-looking older fellows who—

"I'll fetch that for you," said a tall, dark-haired guy in jeans, or at least that's what Louise thought he'd said—to Hazel. The actual words were, "Ah'll fetch 'at for ye," with the intonations in all the wrong places.

While Louise's brain translated, Tall, Dark, and Scottish swiped not Hazel's plain black suitcase, but Louise's larger rainbow-print bag.

"Hold on just a minute," Louise snapped, "you've made a

mistake, and that's my bag."

"She's right, dearie," Hazel chimed in helpfully. "Mine's the plain black."

Dark brows knit over a substantial nose. "According to your e-mail, your bag is all over colors," he said—to Hazel—and he still didn't turn loose of the suitcase.

"*My* e-mail," Louise informed him, "said *my* suitcase bears a pastel spectrum print, which it does. Are you Mr. Cromarty?"

He was a big sort of Mr. Cromarty—Liam's son, probably. Not his grandson, because this guy had crow's-feet at the corners of startlingly blue eyes, and a few signs of wear around his mouth. Broad shoulders, long legs, dark hair in need of a trim.

Not at all what Louise had pictured.

"Aye, I'm Liam Cromarty." He released the suitcase to extend a large hand in Louise's direction. "Welcome to Scotland, Miss Cameron."

"She's not the formal type," Hazel supplied as Louise's hand was enveloped in a warm grasp. "Americans aren't, you know. You can call her Louise. I'm Hazel, by the way."

"Pleased to make your acquaintance, Hazel. Will you be traveling with Miss Cameron?"

Louise had trouble understanding Liam Cromarty amid the bustle and noise of the airport, but she could pick up the hopeful note behind his words.

"Gracious, laddie, no," Hazel said. "Harold would have apoplexies if I left him home alone for one more night, and there's my Harold now. Louise, you enjoy your stay. The Edinburgers are nice enough once you get to know them."

Hazel toddled off, halloo'ing at one of those short, sturdy older fellows Louise had planned on having for her driver. Mr. Cromarty seemed sad to see Hazel go—as was Louise.

"Glaswegians are notoriously friendly," he said, picking up Louise's suitcase. "They can't help it any more than they can help naming half their boys Jimmy. Did she natter your ear off for the entire flight?"

The suitcase weighed a ton and had a perfectly functional set of wheels. Scottish guys wrestled telephone poles. Maybe they liked to haul suitcases around too.

"Hazel nattered both of my ears off, showed me pictures of the house where she grew up in Glasgow, the town where she sells wool goods in the Highlands now, and at least four hundred pictures of the grandkiddies," Louise said.

Wee Harry, wee Robbie, and the baby, Agnes. Somewhere east of Iceland, Louise had even started comprehending what Hazel had said.

"I'm a little tired, Mr. Cromarty. Would you mind slowing down?"

"Flying west is easier," he said, adjusting his stride and angling for the doors. "Coming this way you need a bit of time to find your bearings. Are you hungry?"

He moved with the easy grace of a man who could see over the crowds. Louise was tall—almost five foot ten in bare feet—but Mr. Cromarty had nearly six inches on her.

"I'm not that hungry," Louise said. She was too tired to be hungry. "A bottle of water would hit the spot."

They emerged from the airport into a sunny morning, though Louise's body had been expecting the middle of the night.

"Good God, the light," she whispered.

Mr. Cromarty set down her suitcase. "I can lend you my sunglasses once we get to the car."

"Toto, I don't think we're in Maryland anymore," Louise said, shading her eyes. The light poured from the sky, bright, sharp, brilliant in a way at once welcome and unfamiliar.

Either Mr. Cromarty was used to oddball Americans, or he was patient by nature. Louise spun a full, slow circle, letting that light readjust her circadian rhythm, her mood, her spirit. This was light to wake up the body, mind, heart, and soul.

"I might have to take up painting," she said, assaying a smile at her unlikely companion. "Light like this reveals much."

The morning sunshine showed Mr. Cromarty to be north of thirty by a few comfortable years and to have a smile both sad and friendly. Louise could not recall meeting a man with eyes that blue. Those eyes made her want to work with color again, and not simply with line.

"If you want to paint, you must paint," he said. "You're on your holiday. You should spend it as you please. My family has enough artists that we'll find you an easel, brushes, and paints."

He resumed walking, but paused at a curb. "Get in the habit of looking the wrong way before crossing the street, Miss Cameron, or you'll step out in front of a taxi."

On the sidewalk before Louise a white arrow pointed off to the right, underscored by the words, "Look right."

"This is all very different."

"And you're very tired, also hungry and thirsty. The car's this way."

Louise waited until Mr. Cromarty had stepped off the curb, then trundled after him. He knew where he was going, which was why she'd paid Jeannie for his services, and he was easy to spot in a crowd because of his height.

More than his height, though, the way he moved caught Louise's interest.

Liam Cromarty conserved his energy by staying relaxed. Dancers learned this lesson early in their careers or courted injury. As Louise followed him to a small black Mercedes on the ground level of a covered garage, an extraordinary thought emerged from her tired, travel-fried mind.

She'd like Liam Cromarty to model for her.

— ⁓◌⁓ —

Perhaps Scotland could learn a thing or two from the United States about spinsters.

Liam had traveled extensively in the United States, though, and all his lectures and gallery openings and interviews didn't support the theory that American spinsters were on the whole astonishingly pretty, and grace itself in early morning sunshine.

Louise Cameron wore her height regally. She regarded the world from slanting chocolate brown eyes that hinted of both disappointment and determination. Her mouth required study, not only because her accent held beguiling traces of the American South, but also because she didn't speak much, and Liam didn't want to miss what little she said.

"I won't mind if you want to nod off," he said as they tooled away from the airport. Traffic, fortunately, was inbound toward Edinburgh at this hour, while Liam's destination was to the north.

"I didn't travel 3,500 miles so I could take a nap, Mr. Cromarty. Will we cross the Forth Road Bridge?"

"In about ten minutes, traffic permitting. You'll find water in the glove box."

Liam allowed her a bit of crankiness. International travel wasn't for everybody, and she had to be exhausted.

She cracked open a bottle of Highland Spring still and took a delicate sip. "What do you do, Mr. Cromarty, when you aren't driving Americans around?"

She was an attorney. Of course, she'd ask questions.

"I teach art history and art appreciation." The answer Liam gave even friends and family, though that wasn't all he did.

Another sip of water. Miss Cameron's hands on a mere plastic bottle managed to look elegant.

"Do you have a favorite period or artist?" she asked.

"Many, but mostly I'm drawn to particular works. I noticed you'd like to visit Rosslyn Chapel, for example. It's well worth an afternoon and this early in spring, it won't be crowded." Liam enjoyed Rosslyn Chapel because it was quiet, the setting was lovely, and the grounds always had at least one friendly cat.

Jeannie had passed along an itinerary that was a curious mixture of the predictable and the puzzling: Culloden Battlefield and the Robert Burns museum, but also "Glasgow."

The entire city? The Willow Tea Rooms? The School of Design? What did an attorney want to see in "Glasgow"?

Or, "The Highlands," which, when taken with the islands, comprised more than half of Scotland.

"What sort of law do you practice, Miss Cameron?"

"General practice. In a small town that means wills, divorces, barking dogs, contracts, guardianships. Lots of variety."

This recitation did not animate her as the simple morning sunshine had, but then, what manner of people went to court over barking dogs?

"Are you hungry?" Liam asked.

"Probably."

"You're not in the United States, Miss Cameron. Women are expected to eat in Scotland, and we like them better for it."

Her lips quirked. Because Liam was dodging around a lorry, he couldn't tell if she'd been about to smile or grimace.

"The traffic is all backward here," she said. "The fast lane is the slow lane, and we're on the wrong side of the road, and I'm on the wrong side of the car. I like it."

She wouldn't like the gas prices, but then, the distances were generally much smaller in Scotland than in the Unites States.

"You can give driving a try when we get out to the country," Liam suggested. "In a lot of places, we have only one-lane roads and that simplifies driving considerably."

Miss Cameron was daintily, relentlessly, swilling down the entire bottle of water. Each time she'd twist off the cap, take a sip, then replace the cap snugly on the bottle. Her hands were long-fingered and ringless.

She wore no jewelry, in fact, which was either a visual sort of quietness, or a precaution against airport security delays.

"I want to see the places with one-lane roads," she said. "I want to see cows and sheep too."

The lady was decidedly odd, even for an American. "You

haven't any of those in Maryland?"

"I want to see them *in this light*, Mr. Cromarty, and we don't have those shaggy, red cows with long horns, at least not that I've seen. Those are *cows*, not some prissy bovine selectively bred to produce low-fat milk and six genetically identical calves a year."

From what Liam could recall of his carnivore days, the Highland cow was exceptionally good eating, too.

"The Forth Road Bridge, Miss Cameron, and to the east of us is the rail bridge."

She fell silent as they crossed over the Firth of Forth estuary. To their right was one of the most photographed bridges in the world, a bright red, century-old marvel of engineering and perpetual maintenance. To cross either the rail bridge or the Forth Road Bridge was to leave Edinburgh behind.

Always welcome, that.

"How much farther?" Miss Cameron asked about ten minutes on. The North Sea danced under morning sunshine to their right, while green hills and the occasional farmstead lay off to the left.

"About an hour, all of it pretty. I picked up some scones on the way to the airport. You're welcome to have at them with me."

"Scones," she murmured, apparently going for a Scottish pronunciation. From her, the word came out halfway between "scuns" and "sco-wans," which was nearly spot-on for Perthshire.

"With butter," Liam said. "You'll find a plastic knife in the bag as well. I'll start with cinnamon, and don't spare the butter."

He'd chosen four different varieties—plain, cinnamon, raspberry, and chocolate chip. Miss Cameron slathered butter all over his, then passed it to him wrapped in a serviette.

"But-ter," she repeated under her breath.

Liam took a bite of very good fresh scone. "Are you

mocking me, Miss Cameron? I can show you accents that make mine look like English public school."

Defying both his first and second guesses, she chose plain for herself, though she did apply a decent amount of butter.

"Your voice is like the sunlight to me, Mr. Cromarty. Your accent illuminates vowels and consonants I'd stopped hearing. You make words shine."

Louise Cameron liked the sunlight in Scotland, she liked the driving patterns, and she liked Liam's accent. Perhaps these two weeks wouldn't be such a trial after all.

~ ⦿ ~

Whoever said the occasional modest dose of gluten was bad for the body was an idiot. Louise nibbled fresh-baked heaven, the scone balancing on the edge between bread and pastry, between sinful and delicious.

And the butter had to be organic. But-ter. Mr. Cromarty's elocution was a revelation, a more athletic, energetic rendering of the English alphabet than Louise could muster, plus some vowel sounds she was sure hadn't crossed the Atlantic with the pilgrims.

She opened the second and last bottle of water.

"Thirsty, Mr. Cromarty?"

"A wee nip will do," he said, accepting the bottle from her. The second half of his scone was balanced on his thigh, and he handled the steering wheel and the water bottle easily. No speeding for Mr. Cromarty.

He passed the bottle back, and Louise took a drink before twisting the cap back on. Even the water here tasted—

"Holy Ned," Louise muttered, staring at the bottle. "I can't believe I did that."

Mr. Cromarty maneuvered the car off the four-lane highway and onto a side road.

"Did what? Shared the bottle with me? I'm in good health. We'll be breathing the same air for the next few weeks, touching the same doorknobs. I think you're safe enough,

Miss Cameron."

He was laughing at her. Louise was too tired to smack him, and besides, she hadn't figured out how to drive here yet. Liam Cromarty was necessary to her plans, and she liked listening to him.

"Sharing a bottle is biologically comparable to kissing," Louise said. "I don't kiss guys I've just met, no matter how much I enjoy their vowels."

That was the last thing she recalled saying, until a large hand gently shook her shoulder.

"Wake up, Miss Cameron. Welcome to your temporary home."

Louise was in the middle of preparing a Motion to Reconsider while Robert pranced around the courtroom wearing nothing but a Greek drinking vessel on his head.

"I'm not finished," she muttered.

"The rain will start any minute."

Courtrooms suffered excesses of hot air, but no rain. "Go away."

The next thing Louis knew, she was scooped out of the car and hefted against a broad male chest. Her first instinct was to cuddle up to soft wool and woodsy aromas, but she instead heaved open her eyes.

"You, sir, are carrying me." Carrying her up to a little house snuggled among big trees.

"American ladies are a sharp bunch," Mr. Cromarty said, "but they can't hold their scones worth a damn." He deposited Louise on a padded porch swing, produced keys from his jacket pocket, and opened the door just as thunder rumbled off in the distance.

"Welcome to Dunroamin Cottage, Miss Cameron. The temperature's dropping, and we can't have you falling asleep in the wet."

"Give me a minute, please." Or an hour or an entire season.

The sun had fled behind steely clouds, leaving the cottage

surrounded by gloom and forest primeval. The leaves had a self-illuminated quality visible only as new foliage passed through the chartreuse phase of unfurling.

The surrounding trees were a mix of conifers and hardwoods, and the yard was mostly rocks and bracken.

Mr. Cromarty picked up Louise's suitcase and disappeared into the cottage. The dwelling was cozy, a two-story stone structure that begged for pots of flowers by day and mysterious dancing lights at twilight.

Thunder sounded again, and a chipper, woodsy breeze gusted through the clearing.

"Shall I start you a fire?" Mr. Cromarty asked, closing the door behind him and rejoining Louise on the porch. "The rain wasn't supposed to start until this afternoon, but Scottish weather has a mind of its own."

"I don't want to go inside," Louise said. "I've always loved storms, and one of the things I didn't like about being a lawyer is that I always worked inside."

Though Louise had only now realized that. Long, long days in the courtroom, sitting, sitting, sitting, and trying to stay mentally sharp in an environment budgeted to dull the senses before the morning recess.

No courtroom had *ever* smelled as lush and intriguing as the breeze wafting around this little Scottish cottage. Neither had the drawing studios at the art school.

Mr. Cromarty took the place beside Louise, the chains creaking as the swing dipped.

"Shall I show you the studio now, or would you like to finish that nap you started?"

All the useful pieces of Louise's mind had been flung 38,000 feet in the air, and they weren't floating back to earth in the right order. The lawyer part of her couldn't seem to connect with the art teacher part of her, and neither of those had quite hitched up to her body or her usual sense of organization.

A sensible woman would take a nap—or finish the nap

she'd started.

"Would you sit with me for a few minutes, Mr. Cromarty?" Louise wanted his warmth, wanted that comfortable-in-his-own-skin vibe right by her side.

"This is a pretty place to bide," he said, ranging an arm along the back of the swing. "I have good memories of this cottage. I wrote my doctoral thesis here."

A yes, then. A friendly yes to her request for company.

He was Dr. Cromarty, PhD, but hadn't bothered with the academic title when introducing himself. More evidence that Liam Cromarty knew exactly who he was, and had nothing to prove to anybody.

Whereas Louise—

"Why the sigh, Miss Cameron?" He pushed off with the heel of his boot and set the swing in motion.

"I cannot recall being this tired since finals week my third year of law school," Louise said. "I think I've been tired for a long time, but that plane ride did me in." Or maybe she hadn't had anybody to sit with in years. "What's your PhD in?"

"Art history."

A rosy sense of good cheer took up residence in Louise's middle. Liam Cromarty liked art. How many guys liked art, much less made it their primary area of study?

"I like art too." Good to recall that. At one time, Louise had loved art with a stupid passion.

"Right—you're a potter."

Pot-ter. Once upon a time, Louise had been a *ceramic artist*. The hottest talent to hit the galleries in years, supposedly, though hot talent and galleries struck her as a contradiction in terms now.

"I've thrown some pots. I'd like to do more of that while I'm here." Louise would also like to rest her head on Liam Cromarty's shoulder, but snatched the last scintilla of dignity from her carry-on brain and resisted that temptation.

The wind died as the thunder rumbled yet closer.

"The studio's stocked and waiting for you, Miss Cameron. My cousin Morag works in ceramics, and if her own facilities ever come a cropper, the wheel and kiln here are her backup plan."

"Everybody needs a backup plan. What's a nice PhD like you doing driving tourists around old Scotia? Am I your backup plan?"

The first soft patter of rain hit green leaves, faded, then resurged into a steady downpour.

"You're a favor to my cousin Jeannie, with whom you did most of your corresponding. For the next two weeks I'm between terms, and I know my way around fairly well."

Louise had lost her way. With thousands of miles between her and a cookie-cutter apartment in nearby York, Pennsylvania, she could see that. What she could not fathom was why Scotland should feel so welcoming, irrespective of the man sitting next to her.

"I'll fall asleep if we stay out here much longer."

Mr. Cromarty was off the swing in one lithe movement. "Come along, then. I'll show you around, and you can catch forty winks."

# CHAPTER TWO

Mr. Cromarty extended a hand to Louise, and she took it, though such was her fatigue that when she stood, she needed a moment to get her bearings. He kept her hand in his, until Louise was the one to let go.

The cottage was designed with recessed lighting that brightened up an interior the surrounding trees could have made gloomy. In the kitchen and dining area, which sat to the left of the front door, the floors were flagstone. To the right, the living room had polished oak floors, a fieldstone hearth along the inside wall, and picture windows looking out on the woods.

"The photos on the web site don't do this cottage justice," Louise said. "They don't show the trees, the skylights, the ferns, the books, or,"—the sense of homecoming welled again, higher this time—"*the kitty.*"

Mr. Cromarty left off opening drawers and cupboards in the kitchen.

"So this is where the damned hairy bugger has got off to. Please tell me you're not allergic?" He scooped up what had to be twenty pounds of long-haired black feline from the sofa, and from across the room, Louise heard a stentorian purr.

"I'm not allergic. I like cats." Robert had detested them. Louise suspected he'd been less than gentle with Blackstone when she hadn't been home to referee.

"There's a cat door in back," Mr. Cromarty said, "but I thought I'd locked it shut. Dougie won't be any bother, but I can take him home with me if you'd rather."

The cat booped Mr. Cromarty's chin with his head then turned golden eyes on Louise as if to say, "I saw him first."

"I can use the company," Louise said, stroking a hand over the cat's back. "His name's Dougie?"

"Black Douglas. He ought to be Black Shameless."

Another head boop. Mr. Cromarty loved his shameless cat, and the cat—if ever a cat were to admit such thing—loved Mr. Cromarty.

"Leave Dougie with me," Louise said. "I'm sure he'll find his way home when he's hungry enough."

"Starvation plagues him unceasingly."

Mr. Cromarty didn't turn loose of the cat, but kept him cradled in a purring, contented embrace as Louise was given a tour of the cottage. In addition to the kitchen/dining area and living room, the downstairs held a half bath and a small ceramic studio complete with fridge, kiln, shelves, tools, and a small plastic trash can for clay.

Upstairs was divided into a bedroom that felt like a treehouse—much of the ceiling was a skylight—and a study with computer and reference books. Both the study and the bedroom had floor-to-ceiling picture windows, and from the bedroom a placid river was visible through the trees.

"There's food in the fridge," Mr. Comarty said as they trooped downstairs. "The basics, and a few things Jeannie says are essentials. We can pick up anything else you need tomorrow. You've a charger for your phone and laptop?"

"I do, one for each." Jane and Dunstan had seen to that, and the requisite adapter plugs. "When shall we leave tomorrow?"

Louise had scheduled a trip to the Scottish National Portrait

Gallery, a hike up Arthur's Seat, and a visit to Rosslyn Chapel, none of which would happen unless she was thoroughly rested.

"I'd like to get an early start," she added.

"We'll want to miss traffic, so there's not much point leaving before eight thirty a.m. Does that suit?"

They'd returned to the porch, where the eaves dripped damply, though the rain had either paused or moved on.

"I will probably sleep until then," Louise said, "which seems a shameful waste of a day in Scotland."

Mr. Cromarty shifted the cat to his other shoulder with the ease of a parent handling a sturdy baby.

"You take a nap, Miss Cameron. After an hour or two at most, get up and go for a walk. If you look in the desk drawer in the study, you'll find a map of the walking trails, and the one along the river is mostly level as far as the waterfall. Go for a ramble, check your e-mail—we're five hours ahead of the East Coast—and curl up with a book and a sandwich. That'll set you up for the rest of your stay."

Louise scratched the cat's chin, though that meant sharp claws dug into the shoulder of Mr. Cromarty's jacket.

"You've done this?" she asked. "Flown across the Atlantic?"

"Many times, though not as often in recent years. If you need me, my house is straight out the back, through the trees about fifty yards. You can't miss it, and the door's never locked."

Louise's apartment in York was locked and alarmed, though what would anybody steal? A lot of sketchbooks featuring portraits of her own feet, Robert's hands, or a sleeping Blackstone.

"Thanks, Mr. Cromarty. I'll expect you tomorrow at eight-thirty."

Louise meant to pluck the cat from his shoulder, but Dougie was a cat, and thus her efforts were resisted by virtue of several claws hooked deeply into Mr. Cromarty's lapel.

"Drat the beast," he muttered, trying to extricate the cat's claws one by one. Dougie, however, had no intention of parting with his owner, and grabbed on with his free paw just as the first paw was unfastened.

"Let me," Louise said. "You hold him, and I'll—"

She slid a hand between Mr. Cromarty's jacket and his chest, which was covered with a black T-shirt. The result was a few moments of tactile intimacy nobody—except perhaps the cat—had planned on.

Mr. Cromarty smelled delicious. Against the back of Louise's hand, he gave off an animal warmth, and this close he was pure, solid male. She was hit with a wave of stupidity— fatigue, female awareness of the man she touched, and bewilderment at the entire situation.

"Dougie, let go," Mr. Cromarty growled. "Bad kitties get no tuna fish."

Having destroyed Louise's composure and perhaps some of Mr. Comarty's, the cat turned up docile and cuddled against Louise's middle.

"Stay with Miss Cameron," he said, shaking a finger at the cat, "or I'll throw you in the river where the fishes can make sport of you. You can be our own local river monster."

The cat blinked and, if anything, purred more loudly as his owner thumped down the porch steps.

"Mr. Cromarty?"

He paused amid the rocks and bracken at the foot of the steps, a man whose looks would not substantially change for the rest of his life. Liam Cromarty wasn't exactly handsome, but he was attractive. Very attractive. Also patient, considerate, fond of cats, and interested in art.

"Miss Cameron?"

"Could you—? I mean, I don't know what's expected here. In Scotland. Between relative strangers. And you have to be honest if it's not appropriate. Could you call me Louise?"

"Liam," he said, without an instant's hesitation. His smile

had nothing of the wolf, but it crinkled his blue eyes and lit up his face with a breathtaking warmth. "And I shall call you Louise."

"The American spinster stole your man," Liam informed Helen. She cocked her shaggy head, tongue lolling, but didn't leave her bed.

"We're getting old," Liam said, closing the door behind him. He'd taken the dog for a good hike before going to the airport, but the larger breeds tended to age sooner, and one walk a day was Helen's limit anymore.

"C'mon," Liam said. "Up with you. We're not quite decrepit, and the back porch awaits."

Helen got to her feet, shook her head hard enough to make her big ears flap, and obediently followed Liam through the house to the screened back porch. The rain had left the woods damp, fragrant, and sparkly with midday sun. Rather than go bounding off through the bushes, all Helen did was squat among the bracken and then commence sniffing a few rocks.

"I resent that Miss Cameron has borrowed my cat," Liam told the dog. "You don't appear to miss him."

Helen glanced his way and went back to her investigations. She was mostly deerhound, with some mastiff thrown in and perhaps a bear or two on the dam side.

Liam was debating whether to have lunch or grade the last of the term's papers when his phone rang.

Jeannie. He debated letting the call ring through to voice mail, but she'd simply keep calling and texting until he answered.

"She's here," Liam said, "and likely asleep by now, and yes, I changed the sheets last night." From flannel to cotton, a pattern of roses that smelled of the lavender sachets Jeannie stashed in the linen closet.

"Hello to you too, Liam," Morag said. "Jeannie's putting the baby down, so I'm using her phone. Did you know she and

Harold have been fighting?"

"That doesn't mean they're getting a divorce," Liam said, gently, because Morag was angry in proportion to how badly she hurt, and lately she'd been very angry.

"You've not been married for a long time, Liam," Morag said. "There's fighting and there's fighting. Henry doesn't sleep through the night yet, and nobody fights fair when they're exhausted. What's the latest American like?"

The latest American was tall, pretty, and had a weakness for Scottish vowels of the male persuasion. She would like Liam's back porch, and probably like Helen, too.

"Seems a sensible sort, but then, lawyers often are. Thanks for kitting out the pot shop."

"If she wants more than the basics, send her to me. We'll throw mud together. Jeannie says to tell you Miss Cameron has been to art school."

"Bugger what Jeannie says." Bugger all of Liam's interfering relations, rooting about in his life like Helen on the scent of a rabbit. "Just because a woman has taken a class in throwing pots doesn't mean she'll fancy a fellow who's fascinated by brush work in Low Country Renaissance masters."

Though Miss Cameron—*Louise*—also liked cats. A fine quality in any woman.

"Jeannie wants to see you happy, Liam." Morag's scold was all the more effective for being uncharacteristically gentle.

"For the next two weeks, I'll burn up a fortune in gas, see all the sights we were dragged to repeatedly as children, and pretend yet another loch is the most beautiful scenery on earth." Moreover, Liam would be *cheerful* for those two weeks, because Jeannie had asked this of him. "Enough about my non-holidays. How are you, Morag?"

Liam could do a credible version of the older-cousin inquisition with Morag because he *was* older, and because she'd been away at university for most of the year following Karen's death.

"I'm fine."

Liam could picture the exact "I'm fine" smile Morag wore. Helen growled through such a smile when confronted with a small, male dog intent on taking liberties.

"Jeannie says you've lost weight, Morag."

A pause ensued, during which Morag might have been taking the phone to a more private location—or counting to ten.

"Jeannie is a mother," Morag said. "Their vision changes when they give birth, so everybody looks in need of a meal or three. I think she's fallen asleep with the little rotter, Liam."

Morag was asking a question, as best Morag knew how to ask anything of anybody.

"Don't let her sleep in the same bed as the baby, but before you kidnap Henry off to his crib, tell me how you're doing, Morag Colleen Cromarty."

"I hate you, you know."

"That well?"

"I'm goddamned lonely, Liam. I'm glad to be free of Dean, but I'm lonely. He was at least somebody to resent, and now…" Her voice dropped. "Jeannie said you went a little crazy when Karen died. I can't imagine being this lonely and grieving too. How did you stand it?"

Not well. Not well at all.

"Your vision becomes impaired," he said, as Helen's pale, plumed tail waved among the bracken like a flag of surrender. "You learn not to see very far behind you or in front of you. You do the next necessary thing, and time and pride eventually pull you up out of the ditch."

"I'm making the ugliest gnomes you've ever seen. Nasty little fellows that ought to bring exorbitant sums."

They were probably merry, fat, and cute. "Watch the drinking, love."

"No worries. Can't throw a decent pot when I'm blutered."

Then thank God for Morag's pottery wheel. "Tell Jeannie

the American is fine, and I'll take good care of her."

"I'll tell her the American is a right terror, and this will be the longest two weeks of your life."

"Save me a gnome. Love you, More."

The line went dead.

Liam was something of a thorn in his family's side because he *told* them he loved them. Said the words often and in public, Scottish reticence be damned.

Helen's head lifted, her gaze turning toward the river. Down on the path along the bank, Miss Cameron went marching by.

"Sit," Liam said softly. "We have papers to grade, and we're too old to go chasing after tourists. Besides, she doesn't kiss men she's just met."

And for her scruples, Liam liked her all the more.

---

Robert Stiedenbeck, III, had wanted to remain friends with Louise.

"We're colleagues, too, aren't we, Lou?" he'd asked as he'd packed for New York. "We'll keep in touch, and you can read my stuff for me, the same as always. If you want to visit the Big Apple, our couch is always available."

*Our* couch. His and his Sweet Young Thing's.

Louise had watched him go, feeling as much relief as heartache. Robert had seemed like a good idea at the time, but he'd also reminded her of Dr. Allan Hellenbore, professor of studio arts, seduction, and ceramic forgery. Same friendly, self-mocking arrogance, same quick intellect coupled with an instinct for self-interest that boded ill for anybody else's dreams.

Louise could go for months without thinking of Allan Hellenbore. She'd learn not to think of Robert. Not to be angry at him, not to wonder what in the hell—

The first step toward not thinking about somebody was to not think of them.

"Rise and shine," Louise muttered to the cat plastered to

her side. Dougie lifted his head, stared at her, and stretched to a magnificent length.

"My, what impressive claws you have," she said, dragging the cat onto her belly. Overhead, the skylight framed a leafy canopy, birds flitted, and morning sunshine poured across it all at a low angle.

While in Louise's lavender-scented bed, Dougie was a comforting, warm, rumbly weight.

"I've been here only a day, and already, I know I won't want to go back to York," Louise murmured. "This is not good, Cat. I don't want to teach drawing to a bunch of giggling children. They're either texting their weekend hookup, or convinced they're the next Michelangelo. I'm even more sure I don't want to go back into the courtroom."

That prospect loomed like "backup time," the sentence hanging over a convicted criminal's head if the conditions of parole weren't met. A taste of liberty, and then—a speeding ticket, a little too much to drink—wham, back in the hoosegow.

Dougie took to kneading the sheets.

"You are a good kitty. I like you. You must be hungry." Dougie wasn't a fat cat. He was simply big, all over big, and hairy. "I'll miss you when I leave, and how pathetic is that?"

"Hullo, the house!" a man's voice called.

Dougie sprang from the bed and disappeared into the hallway, tail up, a cat on a mission.

"Gimme a minute!" Louise bellowed back. The clock said 7:45, but perhaps Liam had brought more scones. The leftovers from yesterday were in the fridge, minus the chocolate chippers that had been Louise's dessert and snack.

Also her dinner. One of her dinners. The other had been a grilled cheese-on-rye sandwich.

She slipped into jeans and a T-shirt, then grabbed a flannel shirt for the sake of modesty and padded after the cat.

The guy standing in her kitchen was *not* Liam. "Who are you?"

Bonnie Prince Charlie's grandpa left off munching one of the cinnamon scones Louise had been saving for Liam. He was white-haired, tall, thick-chested, and wore a red plaid kilt along with boots, knee socks, and bright red T-shirt.

"You were fishing yesterday, weren't you?" Louise asked.

He'd been wearing plaid waders—the better to attract Scottish trout?—and singing something about rantin' and rovin'. Louise had stuck to the path and quietly passed by, and when she'd returned, he'd been gone.

"I might ask the same question, lass: Who are you? I see you've passed muster with ma' wee friend Dougie."

Dougie stropped himself against heavy boots, clearly comfortable with the intruder. Louise sensed no threat from the guy, no menace, though the cinnamon scone was rapidly becoming history.

"Did you find the butter?" she asked.

"Aye, thank you, and the coffee's on. I'm Uncle Donald. Welcome to Dunroamin Cottage. I expect you're Jeannie's latest American?" He passed her the box of scones, which held one plain and two raspberry.

Louise had never had an Uncle Donald. Now might be a fine time to acquire one. "If you made coffee, you're welcome to stay," she said. "Did you catch anything while you were fishing yesterday?"

"I'm in the river most days, though I seldom call it fishing. What brings you to Scotland?"

A need to see fairy lights at dusk, and find strange old fellows making coffee in the morning? The coffee maker hissed and gurgled, and a heavenly aroma filled the kitchen.

"I wanted to get away," Louise said, "and I've never been here before. Shall we sit?"

Uncle Donald put whole milk on the table and a bowl of white and brown lumps of sugar. Dougie sat before the fridge, switching his plume-y tail, until Uncle Donald took down a quarter-size green ceramic bowl from the cupboard and filled it with milk.

"The beasts train us, poor dumb creatures that we are," he said, passing Louise the milk and setting out two plates. "You Americans like your orange juice, am I right?"

"Please. Are all Scottish men so well trained?"

"I'm a bachelor," Uncle Donald said. "One learns to fend for oneself."

For an instant, blue eyes focused on Louise, not unkindly, but as if the statement had some significance she wasn't awake enough to figure out.

"Do you drink coffee?" she asked.

"Perish the notion. I drink tea, and whisky, of course." He produced a flask covered in green and blue plaid. "Shall you have a wee nip?"

Whisky in the fudge and whisky for breakfast. No wonder people loved Scotland. "No, thank you."

He tipped back the flask, his wee nip not so wee. "I do love a good island single malt. What's your name, Yank?"

Louise was torn between a sense of privacy invaded, and the novelty of having company for breakfast.

"Louise Cameron, attorney at law, sort of." She could go a-lawyering again if she had to, couldn't she?

"Camerons are thick on the ground here, though they haven't always been popular. Eat, child. Are you and Jeannie off to the city, then? Fine day to see the sights."

Louise dipped a corner of the raspberry scone in her coffee.

"Liam is taking me into Edinburgh today. We're supposed to see the portrait gallery, then tool out to Rosslyn Chapel, and finish with a climb up Arthur's Seat."

Another not-so-wee nip. "Busy folk, you Americans. Shall you put butter on that?" He nudged the butter dish to Louise's side of the table.

She nearly said, "Aye," such was the Scottish gravitational pull of Uncle Donald's company. "The butter here is good."

"The food here is good," he countered. "We don't go for those android crops you make in your laboratories. Our dairy is mostly organic, as is much of our produce. You must also try the whiskys, though Liam won't be much help in that regard."

"You're his uncle?"

"I'm the Cromarty uncle-at-large, more or less. You mustn't mind Liam."

Family was family the world over. Aunt Evangeline had probably said those same words about Louise to half the bachelors in Atlanta. *You mustn't mind Louise. She went to school Up Nawthe.*

"What does that mean, I mustn't mind Liam?" Louise liked Liam, right down to his t's, and d's, and the crow's-feet fanning from his eyes.

"We try to include him," Uncle Donald said, "but the boy's not very includable. Hasn't been since—"

A sharp rap on the door interrupted whatever confidence Uncle Donald had been about to inflict on Louise. Lawyers probably heard more dirty family laundry than therapists did, and she certainly didn't want to hear Liam Cromarty's.

She opened the door to find the man himself on her doorstep. The cat shot out between his legs, while Uncle Donald remained at the table, munching the last of Louise's raspberry scone.

"Uncle, what a surprise." Liam clearly wasn't pleased to see Donald, and neither was he surprised.

"Liam, good day to ye. Help yourself to a scone, and the coffee's hot."

Liam wore a kilt, another black T-shirt, and a wool jacket. The only resemblance between the two men, though, was size and blue eyes.

"I have an aunt just like Uncle Donald," Louise said, patting Liam's chest. "Every bit as presuming, though not half as likable. You might as well have some coffee. I'm not quite ready to leave."

"Liam doesn't eat meat," Uncle Donald observed as he dusted his fingers. "Makes him skinny and cranky, but a day in the city will do the boy good."

"At least I don't housebreak uninvited," Liam remarked, taking up Dougie's empty green bowl and running it under the tap. "You'll cost Jeannie her business one of these days, old man. Miss Cameron's a lawyer. She can sue you for unlawful entry and pilfering her scones."

Liam sounded more Scottish—"auld mon"—and he looked more Scottish in his kilt and boots. He smelled the same, though. Spicy, woodsy, delightful.

"Save me the last raspberry scone," Louise said, "and Uncle Donald, it was a pleasure to meet you—mostly."

With two Cromarty men in the kitchen, the space became significantly smaller. Louise took herself upstairs, grabbed a shower, finished dressing, and came down to find Liam alone, putting the last of the dishes away.

"You can relax," Louise said. "Uncle Donald hadn't really warmed up before you got here, and your deep, dark secrets are safe for now."

Liam draped a red plaid towel just so over the handle to the oven. "You have an aunt like him?"

"She has to let everybody know I graduated first in my law school class, and that business with art school was a funny little idea I picked up from the Yankees, bless their hearts."

Liam stared at the towel, his hands tucked into his armpits. "And every time she says it, you hurt a bit, but you've learned not to show it. I don't drink spirits."

Every time Aunt Evangeline dismissed four years of hard work and heartbreak as a silly little phase, Louise died inside. When Aunt Ev started in on *that awful man* and *the silly business about the pots*, Louise spent days in hell.

"Sobriety is a fine quality in the man who'll be driving me all over Scotland, Liam."

His shoulders relaxed, his hands returned to his sides. "I

enjoy a good ale, and I've been known to have a glass of wine."

The topic was sensitive, though, and personal, so Louise changed the subject. "Do we pack lunch, or eat on the run?"

"We'll eat atop of Arthur's Seat, unless you have an objection to picnicking?"

Louise had not gone on a picnic for... she couldn't recall her last picnic. "No objection at all. Let me grab my jacket and purse, and last one to the car is a rotten egg."

When she joined Liam at the car, he held the door for her, and she climbed in, prepared to enjoy a day that combined art, architecture, exercise, and natural beauty.

Also some company, though who would have thought: Liam Cromarty, that Scottish male monument to relaxed confidence and easy grace, had deep, dark secrets after all.

Liam enjoyed art—sublime art, ridiculous art, functional art, art that struggled, art that failed, art that did both.

The greatest work of art ever conceived, however, was the human female.

He'd forgotten that.

Louise Cameron first thing in the morning was a different creature entirely from Louise striding around the busy airport terminal, Louise making pronouncements about whom she did and did not kiss, and Louise marching down the river trail.

Louise in the morning was sweet, a little creased around the edges, and intriguing. Liam wanted to kiss her, wanted to bury his hands in long skeins of dark red hair, wanted to sit her on the counter and learn the fit of their bodies.

Which, of course, he would not do. Spring was in the air, and he'd been forced into proximity with a pretty woman— who had artistic inclinations, didn't censure a man for avoiding spirits, and was punctual.

She came swinging down the cottage staircase at eight twenty a.m., dewy and neat in jeans, trainers, and a purple-and-green tie-dyed T-shirt. Her hair was coiled into a low bun held up by no means Liam could discern, and she appeared to be free of makeup—probably the secret to her punctuality.

"I've stashed the last two scones in my sporran," he said. "We can finish them off on the way to Edinburgh."

Louise opened the fridge and passed him four eggs.

"Hard-boiled," she said. "Woman does not live by carbs and fat alone, as tempting as the prospect might be—unless you're vegan?"

Damn Donald's big, presuming, well-intended mouth. "I eat eggs and dairy happily and in quantity." Liam had also been known to enjoy the occasional hapless fish when his body craved protein and the menu offered no vegetarian fare.

"My kinda guy," Louise said, tucking an orange into her purse. "Do we have water in the car?"

"We always have water in the car, trail mix and energy bars." Also a first aid kit, a pair of thermal sleeping bags, waterproof matches, and a pup tent, none of which Liam had ever used. "Do you want to practice driving?"

He'd surprised her—also himself, the Mercedes being less than a year old—but he'd pleased her too.

"How about if I take a day to get acclimated and watch the master in action?" she said. "I missed the countryside yesterday, and I don't want to make that mistake again today."

"The countryside is worth a look," Liam said, getting the door. "And you'll have plenty of opportunity to drive."

He, however, had seen the countryside between Perthshire and Edinburgh countless times. He had not seen a woman lick her fingers one by one, when she'd finished her scone.

"Are you happy, Liam?"

*Americans.* "I hardly know you, Louise." Probably the other half of why he'd thought—fleetingly—of kissing her. "Why would I answer such a personal question honestly?"

"It's only a personal question if the answer's no. I'm not happy either, and I don't enjoy admitting it."

Nobody had asked her to. "Sometimes contentment is the

more reasonable goal. Why did you choose the portrait gallery over the National Gallery?"

She allowed him to change the subject, explaining that she wanted the more Scottish collection. Talk wandered to the various galleries in the Washington, DC, area, which were many and varied.

And she knew them well, including their most recent exhibitions.

"Edinburgh looks old," she said when Liam had wedged the Mercedes into a parking space. "But pretty-old, like your grandma. Not tired-old, like you feel after a bad breakup."

She said the damnedest things. Liam's phone buzzed, probably the call he was expecting from Stockholm.

"This is the less old part of town," Liam said. "The New Town, in fact, though if we're to hike Arthur's Seat, we'll nip over to the Old Town."

Liam dealt with his call when Louise took photos of the Walter Scott monument, and as they wandered in the direction of the gallery, he explained aspects of Edinburgh history every schoolboy took for granted. Louise paid attention to his ramblings and to their surroundings. More than once, she simply stood in the middle of the sidewalk, face upturned to the morning sun, eyes closed.

"Do you do that at home?" Liam asked when she opened her eyes. "Do you stop in the middle of the street and gather freckles?"

"I should do it at home. Freckles are where the angels kissed you."

"I suppose you kiss angels on first acquaintance?"

Louis smacked him gently on the arm, smacked him out of his bad mood, as Jeannie or Morag might have. Karen hadn't been a smacker, and she'd valued her complexion.

At the portrait gallery, the punctual, dainty, quasi-Yankee tourist disappeared, and a different woman entirely emerged: quiet, focused, capable of remaining still for long moments before a portrait or bust.

Unfortunately, Liam liked that woman—liked her too—and found himself again speculating about her kisses.

─ ⟨◦⟨°⟩◦⟩ ─

No wonder Scottish men could bebop around in skirts.

They knew *who they were*, knew where their people had set up camp thousands of years ago, knew where they'd stood as the Roman legions had trooped past along the coast, hundreds of feet below the lookouts, and knew where they'd watched as those same Romans had gone scampering back south, willing to leave "the last of the free" to their hills and lochs.

The Scots knew where their battles had been fought, knew who'd won, and who was still losing.

Liam shared local history with Louise as a conscientious host would, but after twenty minutes at the portrait gallery, Louise put her foot down.

"Turn off the history lecture, professor. I don't know what manner of art historian you are, but to me, the joy of a good painting is that it shows us the painter as well as the subject, and sometimes even the entire society in which the painter created. I'd rather spend a good long while with three interesting paintings, than whip by three galleries in the same time. Go read a newspaper or something. You don't have to babysit me."

Liam's chin came up in such a manner that had Louise been a Roman, she would have started her southerly scamper at a dead gallop.

"I have a wee cousin, Louise. Henry cries, he wets, he burps, he does more objectionable things. Him, I babysit. This is a gallery. Here, I frolic."

Liam had a somber version of frolicking, standing before some paintings as if he could hear them, smell them, and slip through time to see the artist applying the paint to the canvas. One portrait in particular, of a brown-haired fellow in plain late-Georgian attire, held his attention longer than any other.

"Who's that?" Louise asked.

"Robert Burns."

"The Auld Lang Syne guy?"

He gave her a look that said clearly, *God spare me from American ignorance.*

"The very one. Shoo. This is an interesting painting. I'm busy. Be off with you."

Louise bopped him on the arm—he'd smiled at her the first time she'd done it, a sweet, surprised, genuine smile—and moved off to some magnificent royal portraits.

There was probably no explaining Scotsmen, but by God, they could paint. The gallery also had a number of busts, and those Louise found as fascinating as the paintings.

"We're behind schedule," Liam informed her when she'd finally reached the limit of what she could absorb. "Rosslyn Chapel closes at five p.m. this time of year, and you don't want to rush your visit. I propose we see the chapel and then take our walk up Arthur's Seat."

"Why didn't you tell me I was running over?" A schedule was important. Law school had taught Louise that, and private practice had taught it to her all over again. Even an art teacher had to be organized, or papers never got graded, office hours weren't kept—

Liam looked off, his expression vintage stoic-unreadable-Scot as a breeze flapped his kilt around knees that also managed to look stoic.

"You were happy, Louise. I didn't want to intrude."

*She had been happy.* Utterly absorbed by symbolism, brushwork, technique, palette, conventions, innovations, politics, images, noses, costumes—captivated by art in a way that renewed and exhilarated even as it drained.

And Liam had *noticed* that she was happy. Louise wished *he* could be happy, and not simply content.

She kissed his cheek and resisted the urge to hug him.

"Thank you, Liam. I had a wonderful morning. Let's grab

a bite, hit the chapel, then do Arthur's Seat."

His smile was shy and a little bewildered. "Right. *Grab* a bite, *hit* the chapel, and *do* Arthur's Seat. Brilliant."

# CHAPTER THREE

Rosslyn Chapel was a cathedral in miniature, a gem of fifteenth-century extravagance intended to ensure the St. Clair family a warm welcome in heaven. Thanks to well-timed preservation work and mention in a little book by Dan Brown, the chapel also welcomed tens of thousands of visitors every year.

"Who's that?" Louise asked when they'd paid their fare and crossed onto the green surrounding the building.

Liam saw nobody but— "That is the chapel cat. I don't know his name."

"Even the chapels have kitties in Scotland. Do you know how lucky you are?"

Louise picked up the cat, a well-fed black beast who, apparently sensible of the relationship between tourist revenue and his diet, began to purr.

The cat also gave Liam a "she likes me best" look.

Dougie had worn the same expression, last Liam had seen him. "I'll be in the building, Louise. No photos allowed inside."

Without setting the cat down, Louise passed him her cell phone. "My first photo in Scotland, and I'm with a handsome, dark-haired man of few words. If you wouldn't mind?"

Liam had held the camera up to his eye before he realized

he'd been teased. "Shall I leave that gargoyle perched on your head?"

"You will do exactly as you please, Liam Cromarty."

He positioned the shot so the blue Scottish sky and the massive stone of the chapel—no gargoyle—formed the backdrop to an image of a smiling woman and a smug cat. The composition was perfect, the sort of balance that often came from careful contrivance, while the content was anything but contrived.

Before Liam handed the phone back, he e-mailed himself a copy of the photo. An art appreciation class could learn a lot from it.

While Louise read every bit of literature inside the chapel, and peered at length at stonework so delicate as to defy modern comprehension, Liam studied *her*.

The lady did nice things for a pair of worn jeans, and she did nicer things for Liam's mood. She had the knack of challenging without threatening, of offering insights instead of hurling them at him, cousin-style.

Rather than intrude on her further acquaintance with the chapel, Liam went outside, found a sunny bench, followed his phone call from Stockholm with a text to Copenhagen, and then took out the latest of the many art periodicals he tried to keep up with.

He was slogging through another attempt by Robert Stiedenbeck, III, to be profound and witty on the subject of fur as symbolism in American colonial portraiture when Louise joined him on the bench.

"I suppose you've seen the chapel a dozen times?" she asked.

"At least, and I'll see it a dozen more. When I teach in Edinburgh, we bring the class here. The chapel makes an excellent starting point for discussions of the economics of art, and how art can make a different contribution to society as that society changes over centuries."

"They stabled horses in there during the Reformation," Louise said as the cat leaped onto the bench. "Horses, Liam. One swift kick from a cranky mare, and wham, a detail on a carving somebody labored two years to create could have been gone."

Americans had had a revolution and a civil war, but without the oppression of a state religion, they were baffled by the complexity and violence of the Reformation.

The cat walked right into Louise's lap, with the same casual dignity as old ladies walked onto the ferry at the conclusion of an afternoon's shopping.

Liam offered the cat a scratch to the nape of its neck. "Fortunately, the mares were either equine Papists or more interested in their hay than architecture. What is it with you and cats?"

"Have you ever been to Georgia?"

"I have. Friendly place." And the food, holy God, the food... Fried heaven, even for a vegetarian, though the accent was baffling.

"I grew up there. Everybody's nice, but nobody's real, and then,"—she cradled the cat against her shoulder—"they can slice you to ribbons, all the while blessing your heart, darlin', and you poor thang, and that is such a shame-ing. I'm convinced the mixed message was invented by women of the American South."

"Family can be a trial." Liam had the sense Louise's family was worse than that. They were an ongoing affliction that bewildered her and wouldn't go away, like persistent grief.

"I grew up with cats," she said. "Cats are honest. If they don't want you to pick them up, they hiss and scratch. I love them for that. Love that they are simply what they appear to be, and if they enjoy your company, they are honest about that too."

Liam enjoyed Louise's company. He ought not. She wasn't precisely reserved, though she wasn't quite friendly either.

"Georgia is far away," Liam said, closing the periodical. "Family often means well as they're wreaking their havoc, and if you're lucky, they find somebody else to plague with their good intentions before you've committed any hanging felonies. Have you seen enough?"

Louise set the cat on the ground, and the beast went strutting off to its next diplomatic mission for the Scottish tourist industry.

"Your family was hard on you?" Louise asked.

She was a perceptive woman, so Liam gave her a version of the truth.

"I went through a bad patch a few years back. One of those bad breakups you mentioned earlier, followed by a bit too much brooding for a bit too long. They worried."

If Louise regarded that as an invitation to pry, Liam would have only himself to blame, because he never disclosed even that much. He'd done a bit too much drinking, too.

She picked up his magazine, a quarterly journal useful for inducing sleep or lining Dougie's litter box. Liam intended to cancel his subscription, but hadn't got 'round to it.

"You seem to have found your balance now," Louise said. "You read this stuff?"

"I read the abstracts. Somebody needs to teach most academics how to write. The article I attempted was worse than usual, though the learned Dr. Stiedenback will cite it at every lecture he gives for the next three years."

Louise made a face, as if the milk had turned. "You know him? This is an American journal."

"The art world is small, especially the gallery art world." And that world was the last topic Liam wanted to discuss with Louise Cameron. "Do you ever visit those people in Georgia?"

"Every other Christmas. They tsk tsk over all the boyfriends I don't bring along, cluck about the New Year being full of new opportunities, and tell me I'm nothing but skin and bones."

Well, no actually, she wasn't. "They're of Scottish descent, then?"

Ah, a smile. At last another smile. Part of Liam had been waiting hours to see that smile, and now the image he beheld— pretty chapel, pretty spring day, pretty lady—went from well composed to lovely.

"You're hilarious, Liam Cromarty. As a matter of fact, they are Scottish on my father's side. Mom's DAR royalty— Daughters of the American Revolution—and related to Robert E. Lee, too. Daddy is the reason my sisters and I ended up with middle names like Mavis, Fiona, and Ainsley."

"Good names." Beautiful names. "Shall we head back to town? The temperature will drop as the sun sets, and Arthur's Seat can be windy."

Louise passed him the periodical and stood. "You really think that Professor Stiedenbeck doesn't write well?"

Odd question, but at least she wasn't interrogating Liam about his family.

"Somebody has taken pity on the bastard and assigned him a decent editor this time around, but he offers nothing original and takes a long-winded, self-important time to do it. Not very professional of me, but I imagine he's the sort who lectures his lovers into a coma before he gets on with the business, and then doesn't deliver much of a finish."

Lovely became transcendent as Louise fought valiantly against Liam's unprofessional humor and lost, heartily, at length, in happy, loud peals. She was still snickering when they got back to the car, and Liam was smiling simply because he'd made her laugh.

"Cromarty, please don't ever become an art critic," she said, opening a bottle of Highland Spring. "With analysis like that, you will develop a following wide enough to end the career of anybody you take into dislike."

Liam pulled out of the car park, and when Louise offered him a sip from the bottle, he politely declined.

—⁓◦⁓—

Long-dormant powers of observation and analysis stirred inside Louise as she and Liam trekked up the eight-hundred-foot hill flanking Edinburgh to the southeast. The views were lovely, of course, but the terrain, like what she'd seen of Perthshire, wasn't much different from Maryland between the Appalachians and the Chesapeake shores.

And yet…

"I see differently here," Louise said as they stood aside to let an older couple coming down the slope pass them. "I'm noting the details, the colors, the relationships, the geometry. Maybe it's the light."

"Maybe you're on holiday," Liam countered, starting up the trail. "You got a good night's sleep, you're in different surrounds, and you're paying attention. One of the advantages of travel."

Louise paid attention to *him*, and not only because from a three-hundred-word abstract, he'd described Robert Stiedenbeck, III, exactly.

"Men move differently in kilts," Louise said, scrambling up a set of natural rock steps. "More freely. It's attractive."

Even the older guys with their walking sticks and stolid ladies at their sides moved with a certain assurance, but then, so did many of the unkilted men.

And all of the ladies.

"I was hoping I'd hate it here," Louise said, because clearly, Liam wouldn't dignify her comment about the kilts with a reply. "I'm not hating it."

"Hating is a lot of effort. Mind your step."

Liam needed to work on his charm, but he could hike the hell out of a Scottish hill.

"There are no guardrails here," Louise said, taking Liam's proffered hand to negotiate another natural incline. "No signs all over the place. Climb at Your Own Risk, or No Littering, or All Dogs Must Be on a Leash, or Scoop Your Poop."

No litter either. Nobody taking stupid risks.

Liam tugged her over a scattering of loose rock. "Sounds like a lot of noise and blather. How could you see the pretty landscape for all those lectures and scolds?"

Liam's question brought them to a stretch of gently rising grassy slope.

"Stop, please," Louise said, keeping hold of Liam's hand lest he conquer the summit on the strength of forward momentum alone.

He obliged as a quartet of teenagers went giggling and flirting past. "You're in need of a rest?"

"How could I see the pretty landscape for all those lectures and scolds?" Liam's words caught in Louise's throat as she repeated them. "Lectures about posture, deportment, the family name. Lectures about appearance, the right people. Lectures delivered with the arch of an eyebrow or a serving of pecan pie." Her breathing hitched, as if her lungs had been squeezed by a giant, familial hand. "Crap and a half, I thought I was done with all this."

Liam didn't drop her hand, and his grip was reassuringly warm. "Has your family come to call?"

He was quick—the Scots would call him canny—and his gaze was kind.

Louise managed a nod. "Anxiety along with them. I almost never have these episodes anymore. Damn."

She'd learned to breathe through the dread, to count her breaths instead of hoard them. She didn't have panic attacks. She had *episodes*, or—Auntie Ev had of course chimed in—*little spells*.

"Let's sit, shall we?" Liam suggested. The trail was flanked by boulders and rocky outcroppings in spots. He drew Louise over to one, and she sank against it. Liam came down beside her, right immediately beside her.

And he kept her hand in his.

"I'm sorry," Louise said, while the predictable elephant tried to sit on her chest. "New places, schedule whacked. Should have been more careful." Mention of Robert, when he was supposed to be thousands of miles away, lecturing another, younger, more confident woman into a coma, probably hadn't helped either.

Liam rubbed his thumb back and forth across Louise's knuckles. "You should be *less* careful. Enough new places and pretty views, and you'll get your heart back, but that takes time."

And courage. "You speak from experience?"

His thumb slowed. A dog that looked like Irish wolfhound-lite sniffed at Liam's knee, then went trotting off toward the top of the hill.

"I speak from experience, and from hope. Bad things happen, but then there are friendly dogs, beautiful portraits, delicious curries, and lovely views. There's wee Henry, whom I will spoil shamelessly exactly as I do his cousins. There's meaningful work, and a good sturdy piece of granite to oblige us when we're a bit winded."

*A bit winded.* Louise dropped her forehead to Liam's shoulder, as the certainty that all creation faced imminent doom faded, replaced by a simple lump in her throat.

"Were you a bit winded, after your bad breakup?" she asked.

"I was flat knackered, but I'd already been going too hard and too fast for too long."

"I've left the profession that was supposed to be my salvation," Louise said. "I've moved, ditched a relationship that wasn't right, and I have no idea where I'm going." And she'd been going at the lawyer stuff too hard and too fast for the five longest years in the history of lawyering, too. Trying to build a practice, trying to be a solid partner to Jane, who'd been born quoting *Marbury v. Madison.*

Liam's arm came around Louise's shoulders in a bracing squeeze. "Catch your breath, and we'll take the last part slowly. The hill isn't going anywhere, and we still have some light."

For one more moment, Louise had the blessed pleasure of Liam's hand in hers and his arm around her shoulders in a friendly hug. Then he stood, though he remained beside her.

Louise gave herself the space of three more slow, medium breaths—deep breaths could lead to hyperventilation—then got to her feet.

"I'm not going back to Georgia for Christmas," she announced. "Not this year, maybe not ever. Travel at the holidays is crazy, and I can see my sisters anytime." Especially now that her life wasn't ruled by the almighty court docket—though the academic calendar could be just as tyrannical.

"Onward, then," Liam said.

He had the knack of companionship, of neither leading nor following, but staying mostly at Louise's side. When the trail narrowed, he might go first, or Louise might. They didn't need to talk about who led or who followed or which fork to take when they faced a choice.

Because the afternoon was well advanced, the very top of the hill was mostly deserted. They passed the occasional couple or family on a picnic blanket, or a lone walker contemplating a view, but at the highest, rockiest point, they had the hill to themselves.

The North Sea glistened off to the northeast, while beyond Edinburgh, green countryside stretched inland around the Pentland Hills. Louise got out her phone, wanting to capture the memory of a wonderful day.

Despite the visit from her relatives.

"You're smiling," Liam said. "Shall I take a photo?"

"Please, and try not to put any gargoyles in my hair."

The same big, wire-haired dog came sniffing up the rocks, only this time his examination of Liam's knee was cursory. As Liam fiddled with the phone, the dog came panting to Louise's side.

"You smell the chapel kitty," Louise said, offering her hand for inspection. The dog licked her wrist, then took a seat at her feet as if photobombing was all part of the service, ma'am.

"The local Scottish Tourism Board representative wants his picture taken," Liam said as the camera clicked. "I expect the chapel cat sent him. You might smile now, Louise. Scottish deerhounds can be particular about the company they keep."

Louise smiled, because *she* was particular about the company she kept. No more Roberts—he had been a weak moment brought on by a career transition and a sexual drought—and no more pecan pie topped with mixed messages.

For the next two weeks her company would be Scotland and Dougie.

Also Liam Cromarty.

"I think I'll get a dog," she said. "A nice big, friendly dog." Blackstone would have to adjust, or join Jane and Dunstan's practice.

"I like dogs," Liam replied, as the camera clicked again. The breeze whipped his dark hair every which way, but his concentration as he tapped the screen was unwavering.

Down the hill, somebody whistled, and the deerhound trotted off.

"Your turn," Louise said, taking the phone from him. "Think Scottish thoughts."

"Just for that, I'll introduce you to tablet," Liam said, shifting so the wind blew his hair back, not into his eyes. "Or Jeannie's whisky brownies."

"You're talking to a Southern woman, Cromarty. Don't make me get out my bourbon cake recipe."

Viewing him through the camera lens, Louise had to both look and see. What aspect of this guy belonged in his portrait? What would those painters whose works hung in the gallery do with this subject?

Louise shifted the angle, so wide blue sky got honorable mention, along with the cairn of red-brown rocks topping the summit. The sea shone behind the hill, a flat, silver mirror saying farewell to the late-day sun.

And yet the kilted man standing off-center in the frame dominated the image easily.

"What's tablet?" Louise asked.

Just as she hit the shutter button, Liam smiled. Not a Scottish Tourism Board grin, not a pained male, "for God's sake, get it over with" smile.

"You would probably call tablet fudge," he said, with a hint of a challenge. "Sort of a blend of sweetened condensed milk and butter. The perfect treat to tide you over until supper, and I have some in my sporran."

Louise took a second shot of that slight, diabolical smile, but the fiend had dangled a lure her blood sugar couldn't resist. She put her phone away.

"What do I have to do to get some of this magical treat?" she asked.

They were alone at the top of Arthur's Seat, the light would soon fade, and Louise did not want to leave. The views were magnificent, and the climb—and the company—had done her good.

Liam dug in his sporran and passed her a bite-sized square the color of turbinado sugar.

"What you must do to earn this treat, Louise Cameron, is enjoy it."

The texture was perfect, between fudge and hard frosting, the sweetness underlain with the richness of cream. Hot, strong coffee would hold up to such a delectable morsel.

"This stuff ought to come with a gym membership," Louise said. "Chunky Monkey pales by comparison. You aren't having any?"

"My treat," Liam said, brushing a loose strand of hair back from her jaw, "is that right at this moment, you're happy. Tablet is not as delectable as the smile you're wearing, Miss Cameron."

On that unexpected bit of gallantry, he moved off down the incline.

Louise finished her tablet, munching slowly, letting the pleasure dissolve on her tongue as the sun sank lower and the sea gleamed on the horizon.

"I'm happy," she whispered, letting the realization replace all the anxious, dark, doubting feelings she often carried around inside. More baggage than she realized, heavier than she'd known. She lifted her arms to the sky, not caring if Liam was watching.

*I'm happy.*

When she'd clambered down to the path, she fell in beside Liam, content to walk beside him all the way back to the car park. The day had been magical, and some of the magic clung to her, even as she wondered:

What would it take for Liam to be happy too?

—◦◦◦—

A prediction of rain saved Liam's sanity, for yesterday's frolics had about done him in. He took himself down the path to the cottage, intent on confirming with Louise that she'd not need her driver for the day.

Honesty compelled Liam to admit that Louise Cameron's *mouth*—a perfectly mundane arrangement of two lips—had about done him in. Her mouth had moods— thoughtful, determined, merry, frustrated. He'd taken to studying her mouth when he ought to have been studying portraits of old Rabbie Burns or Mad King George.

Louise was leaving in less than two weeks, but the image of her smiling atop Arthur's Seat would linger in Liam's memory long after her departure. More excellent composition, which he'd e-mailed to himself, but he'd probably not share those photos with his classes.

He knocked on the front door of the cottage, and nobody answered. From the base of the picture window, Dougie blinked up at him.

"I brought cat food," Liam informed his pet. "Though I suspect you've wheedled cheese and worse from the lady."

Dougie replied with a squint—a self-satisfied squint.

The door was unlocked, practically guaranteeing another visit from Uncle Donald. "Anybody home?" Liam called as he walked into the kitchen.

Perhaps Uncle Donald had kidnapped Louise for a spot of fishing. She had Liam's cell phone number, and might have called if her plans—

Somebody was down the hall in the studio, humming along to the strains of "Caledonia."

*Bless the rainy forecast.* Liam set the can of gourmet cat food on the kitchen counter, slung his damp jacket around the back of a chair, and eased down the hall.

Louise sat before the pottery wheel, a small column of wet, reddish clay rotating slowly between her hands. Liam's reaction was immediate, erotic, and inconvenient as hell.

He was going daft. First her mouth, then her hands. She pressed her thumbs into the top of the column, creating the beginnings of a dished shape, then continued to press, so the column developed a hollow interior.

Just like Liam's mind. Arousal, visual pleasure, consternation, and surprise rocketed about inside him, but nothing as coherent as an actual thought.

"I know you're there, Liam," Louise said as the clay became a vase. "I thought I heard the door, and I can smell your aftershave. You're allowed to watch. I'm not one of those artists who throws mud at someone who interrupts her work."

From the CD player, Dougie MacLean—*such* a helpful fellow—sang gently about kisses, love, and going home.

"Wouldn't fiddle music be easier to work to?" Liam asked, leaning on the doorjamb. "There's a Paul Anderson album in that stack that's breathtaking."

Everything Paul Anderson recorded was breathtaking.

Louise used the back of her wrist to scratch her chin and got a daub of wet clay on her jaw.

"I'll listen to them all before I leave, possibly before the day's done. The forecast said rain for most of the day."

And thunder and lightning behind Liam's sporran, apparently. For years he'd not been plagued with unforeseen arousal, with much of any arousal. His equipment functioned, he made sure of that from time to time, but Louise with her wet hands and her hair in a haphazard topknot had ambushed him.

"If you want to spend the day here, I have plenty of work to do," Liam said. "Papers to read, lecture notes to prepare. If you need anything, you have only to—"

"I need a hard-boiled egg or two and a cup of coffee."

Liam nearly told her, as he would have told any sister, cousin, or other presuming female, to get it herself or at least say please, but Louise hadn't looked up from her project. She bent closer to the wheel, shaping the vase into a taller column, gently, gently, then spreading the base with the same deft, sure movements.

*She's happy.* She was once again happy.

"You've done this a lot," Liam said. Louise did it well, too. Her expertise was evident in her focus and in the results of her efforts. Some people had the gift of creating art directly with their hands—no brushes, knitting needles, or musical instruments required. They had art—vision, texture, composition—in their very touch.

Louise apparently owned that gift, an ability that went beyond talent to the very nature of the beast doing the creation.

"Used to stay up all night, throwing and re-throwing the same clay. If clay worked for God, why not for a high school kid dragging around thirty extra pounds in all the wrong places?"

More self-disclosure, or another nod to the Georgia pecan pie mafia. "I'll fetch you an egg and a cup of tea."

"I asked for—damn it to hell and back. I'll need all day to learn this wheel. I asked for coffee."

"I don't know how to work that fancy machine," Liam said,

and his ability to read directions was none too reliable at the moment. The smudge on Louise's chin was driving him 'round the bend. "Jeannie bought the coffee maker for a couple of German engineers who visited over the winter."

Then too, tea might steady Liam's nerves.

Without looking up, Louise smiled at her vase and let it pirouette on the wheel for a few rotations, delicacy and dirt dancing together. Then she demolished it, smushing it back onto the wheel with both hands so a formless lump of wet mud twirled off-center where art had been.

"Tea then," she said, using a tool that resembled a wire garrote to free the clay from the wheel. "And some of that tablet stuff you keep in your man purse."

"Sporran," Liam muttered, leaving the lady to her mud. He considered stopping off in the loo, he was that randy, but turned his thoughts to making tea, peeling three hard-boiled eggs, and slicing some cheddar made on the Isle of Mull— island cows were happy cows, according to Jeannie.

The tablet, he left in his sporran, for now.

"Breakfast," he said, setting a tray on the studio's work table a few minutes later. On the CD player, Mr. MacLean had mercifully switched to a pair of fiddles waltzing along in slow harmony.

"All I need is a bite," Louise muttered, leaning far enough forward that a loose hank of hair dropped forward over her shoulder.

An inch more forward and that hair would hit the wheel, which was arguably dangerous and certainly messy. Liam caught the errant lock and tucked it back among its mates.

"Thanks," Louise said, coaxing the clay upward. "This clay acts like it's cold, but it's not. We're having a discussion, the clay and I, or maybe an argument."

Liam held Louise's mug of tea up to her mouth. She took a sip, peering at him over the rim. The smudge of clay on her chin was drying to pale dust, and he wanted to brush it off so badly his fingers itched.

"A bite of egg?" he asked.

"I see you put salt on the tray. I like a sprinkle of salt on mine, please, but just a sprinkle."

As the clay twirled endlessly on the wheel, Liam suffered the torture of feeding the artist by hand. She nibbled delicately from his fingers, the intimacy endurable only because Louise was apparently oblivious to it.

Her attention had been seduced by a lump of wet clay, while Liam eyed the clock and wished the call he expected from Ankara would come in.

Though the image of Louise and the chapel cat had become his phone's wallpaper. Not very smart, that.

"You're an art historian," Louise said as a lovely fluted bowl was obliterated on the spinning surface. "Are you also an artist? I'll teach you to throw in return for driving lessons."

"I dabble with a sketch pad, but I haven't any real talent." Karen had assured Liam of that, but only in recent years had he ignored her laughing assessment and drawn anyway. "Would you like more egg?"

"Cheese first," she said. "I can smell it even in here. I love cheese."

"What happened to the thirty extra pounds?" Liam asked. Louise had found good homes for some of those pounds, in all the right places.

"My older brother got me a horse. Six months of practically living at the barn, and no more thirty extra pounds. I was mostly out of shape, sitting at the wheel by the hour when I wasn't sitting in classes at school, or sitting at my desk doing homework—"

Liam held the lightly salted egg up to Louise's mouth. She took a bite, then another.

"What happened to the horse?" he asked, mostly out of desperation.

"When I went to college, my parents gave me the choice

of selling the horse or passing him along to my sister. I went off to school, and by Christmas, Bobo had been sold. My mother claimed my sister lost interest. My sister claimed Mom wouldn't drive her out to the barn."

Liam held up the egg again, and Louise's attention shifted from what had possibly been the beginning of a teapot to the food.

Liam didn't think. He let protectiveness, sexual arousal, and a need for her to not ignore him drive his actions. When Louise turned toward the half an egg Liam held, instead of the egg he gave her a kiss.

"To hell with Georgia, Louise. If you were happy at the horse barn, sign up for lessons again. You're happy throwing. Set up your studio again. Teach other people to throw. Finish that art degree."

She remained right where she was, her mouth an inch from Liam's.

"I did." She kissed him back, then resumed tormenting her clay, as if people kissed in the course of discussion with her all the time. "I got the damned degree, a lot of good it did me. Tea?"

This art degree had made her unhappy, or perhaps art degrees didn't go well with pecan pie and controlling parents.

While lawyering hadn't gone well for Louise?

"Losing that weight, learning to ride, gave you strength your family wasn't accustomed to seeing in you," Liam said.

"Growing four more inches didn't hurt either," Louise replied, scraping the clay off the wheel. This time she shut the wheel off, so it spun gradually to a halt. "Your tea will get cold, Liam."

She picked up his cup in her wet, muddy hands and held it up to this mouth. He drank despite the incongruous scents of wet clay and roses blending with an understated Darjeeling he'd found in Edinburgh.

"I didn't mean to interrupt your work," Liam said. "You'll

want to converse with your clay, and I'm sure—"

She took a drink of his tea. "I need to think about the clay. I've thought about something else, too, though. I've thought about taking you to bed."

# CHAPTER FOUR

Scottish men were supposed to be hot, fun, and emotionally unavailable. Liam wasn't exactly fun, and he ignored his own sex appeal so thoroughly Louise might have blinked and missed it.

But emotionally, he paid attention. He listened, he saw, he thought about the information he took in. Careful he might be, also shy, reticent, and probably snake-bit—he'd mentioned a bad breakup—but he was emotionally more present than any guy Louise had spent time with since, well, Bobo.

Louise had thought about Liam Cromarty all night, just as, long ago, she might have imagined the last piece of pecan pie in the pantry. What the hell good was being on the rebound if she let the only guy to hold her attention in years go hiking out of her life without even letting him know she wanted to peek under his kilt?

"I have a theory," Liam said, setting his tea cup down in the precise middle of its saucer. "The standard wisdom is that American girls are easy."

He leaned back against the heavy worktable, looking like a relaxed, kilted cover for a men's magazine, right down to drinking his tea from a cup with a saucer under it.

"I'm not a girl." Nor was Louise in the mood for a morality lecture. "If you're not inclined, professor, a simple 'no thank you, pass the salt,' will do. I'm interested, I'm not easy." When nobody asked, a woman had no opportunity to *be* easy.

"Louise Cameron, I have noticed that you are no longer a girl."

Louise got up to wash her hands, the better to turn her back on Liam's rejection.

"I have noticed," Liam went on, "that you are an intelligent, interesting woman to whom I am attracted. You're also quite pretty, but a man never knows if he's supposed to mention a woman's appearance."

And next would come... the *but*. Liam would walk out the door, and Louise would never see him again. Some other handsome, smiling Cromarty would appear in a different vehicle, to do some Nessie-spotting or tour the nearest whisky distillery with her.

Louise resisted the urge to flick water at Liam. She instead did a very thorough job of washing the mud from her hands.

"I've never invited a guy into my bed before, Liam Cromarty. I don't expect I'll make a habit of it."

Because guys like him didn't come along very often. Not in her life. Louise got the slick, smart, dishonest kind instead. The users who never paid a price for their lack of honor and were proud of their guile.

The bow that held Louise's smock up came undone as she turned off the tap.

"You don't kiss strangers, Louise. I've long since outgrown any interest in disporting with easy women."

Liam spoke directly against Louise's bare nape, a stern, talking kiss that sent a lovely shiver through her. He'd taken off his leather purse thing, which he usually wore front and center over his kilt. His arousal was front and center now, snugged against Louise's backside.

"I like you, Liam. I respect you. I also desire you." More

than that, Louise *trusted* him. He'd never casually assume she'd provide free editorial services for his stupid, stilted articles while he packed up to move in with another woman.

Another warm, lingering kiss, this one to the juncture of Louise's shoulder and her neck.

"I'm out of practice, Louise, but I like you and I respect you, too."

And holy God, could Liam use his mouth. He tasted, he teased, he nibbled, he bit Louise's earlobe *just right*, he slid his hands around her middle, and Louise would have cheerfully put the work table to use despite a lovely bed available on the next floor up.

"If you'll put away the clay," Liam said, patting her bottom, "I'll feed the cat and lock the door. Uncle Donald is ever fond of the sneak attack."

Louise managed a nod, grateful for a few minutes to compose herself—and to anticipate the rest of the morning in bed with Liam.

*❧*

As Liam locked *and* dead-bolted the front, back, and side doors, he inventoried his internal security system, looking for panic, dread, second thoughts, anything that suggested intimacy with Louise Cameron was a bad idea.

"It's a messy idea," he told Dougie as he spooned wet food into the green bowl. "A complicated idea. Also irresistible."

Liam petted the cat, who went noisily and enthusiastically facedown into the dish of food.

"Maybe that's why I want to give it a go," he said softly. "One small ocean will limit my folly to two weeks fondly remembered."

He'd spoken the truth, though. He liked Louise and respected her. A lot. Far more than he'd liked the several encounters he'd allowed himself since Karen's death.

Louise had good timing, among her many other fine qualities.

"If she'd left the overtures to me," Liam said, "I'd have been putting her on that plane in two weeks, wondering what might have been and kicking myself for not—"

Louise came striding into the kitchen. "I fed Dougie before I got started this morning. He'll be sleeping off a tuna drunk, and that's a good thing." She kept coming across the kitchen, until she was smack up against Liam, her arms twined around his neck. "You never did tell me your theory."

Liam's theory was they should go upstairs immediately. "What theory?"

"About American women being easy."

That theory. "American women aren't any easier than any other variety of women," Liam said, as Louise led him down the hallway. "But American men are lazy, inconsiderate, incompetent louts. Their women get lonely and restless, and then some handsome, charming fellow sashays by while the lady's on her holiday—we need my sporran."

"And here I was hoping you'd lose the kilt."

Liam looked down at his oldest, plain black work kilt. The one he'd worn for the marathon writing sessions on his dissertation.

"I'm quite partial to this kilt."

"I meant, *take it off*, Liam." Louise swayed up the stairs ahead of him, a delectable sight in black yoga pants and a man's plain white T-shirt. Clay smudged the hem over one hip, and Liam would have bet his autographed first edition of Janson's *"History of Art"* that Louise wasn't wearing a bra.

He wanted to sketch her, smudges and all; wanted to see her throw pots naked; wanted to—fetch his sporran. When Liam got upstairs, Louise stood fully clothed by one of the picture windows, looking out on damp green woods.

"Good," Liam said. "I want to undress you. I want to take down your hair, want to—what?"

"Now you turn up loquacious and take-charge? What if I want to undress you first?"

In the midst of the rainy woods, the sun shone in Liam's heart, and quite possibly a few other locations. He tossed his sporran on the night table.

"Then Louise Cameron, be about your stated agenda, if you please."

She let Liam get his boots off, but then she sat him on the bed, drew his T-shirt over his head, and treated him to the same focused attention Dougie showed his victuals.

"You work out," she said, running her hands over his chest. Her touch was inquisitive and sure, as if he were fresh clay, warm and ready for the wheel and her creative impulses. "But you don't push it with the weights. I like that."

Louise also liked kissing. She'd used her toothbrush while Liam had fed the cat, and she used her imagination as she knelt between Liam's legs and sank her hands into his hair. Her kisses were by turns delicate, plundering, curious, and even shy.

As Liam kissed her back, he waited for the desolation to well, for the sure conviction he was making a fool of himself, for the despair that could rob him of all pleasure.

Louise eased away, arms about his waist, cheek pillowed on his thigh. "I want to savor you, Liam, and I want to throw you on the bed and have at you in case I lose my nerve."

He took the elastic from her hair and set it beside his sporran. "Does that happen? You get this far and wish you'd never asked or accepted?" Did it happen to her *too*?

She nuzzled his parts through the wool of his kilt, an overture as friendly as it was arousing.

"I don't get asked. My brother says I have a No Vacancy light on. You?"

"A widower probably has his own version of the No Vacancy sign. I'm not having second thoughts, Louise. I want to make love with you."

Liam wasn't having second thoughts yet, and didn't sense any lurking. Interesting and a significant relief, or maybe the simple result of accepting overtures from a woman who'd leave in two weeks.

Louise sat up and went to work on the buckles of Liam's kilt. "I didn't know you were a widower, Liam. I'm sorry. Are you all right?" Was he all right? A prosaic, mundane question to which most people expected an equally prosaic reply. Louise unfastened the kilt and flipped the sides open, leaving Liam sitting naked on the bed, Louise kneeling before him.

"I'm doing better. We'll talk."

Because with Louise, Liam could talk. She had a meddling, sometimes insensitive family; she'd made poor career choices; and uncertainty still tried to occasionally steal her breath and her confidence. None of that had followed her up the stairs, and yet it was all a part of who she was and why she appealed to him.

When she stood, Liam pushed her yoga pants off her hips, revealing long legs, interesting knees, and an absence of underwear. Louise picked the yoga pants up with her toes and foot-flung them onto a chair.

"Good aim," Liam remarked, settling his hands on Louise's hips. The artist in him tried to find the right term for the color that was two shades darker than auburn as he coaxed Louise to straddle his lap. While he wrestled with that aesthetic challenge, Louise pulled her T-shirt off and fired it in the direction of the chair too, so they were both naked.

"You don't have to finesse this, Liam. I'm wound up enough—"

He kissed her. "Maybe the problem is, American women don't expect enough of their men, or don't take the time to show the poor blokes how to go on."

And yet, Liam understood Louise's dilemma. She was dealing with a resurgence of desire, a gale-force wind gusting through her mature, rational self-image and her firmly entrenched low expectations. She'd grown accustomed to desire wafting past her life on breezes and zephyrs, not this hurricane of desire and need.

Liam rose with Louise in his arms, her legs twining around his flanks.

"Wall sex?" she asked. "It's fine if you like—"

He tossed her onto the bed. "You tell me, Louise. If you want wall sex, floor sex, doggie sex, oral sex, shower sex, *ceiling* sex—now you're laughing at me, and my charms on display for all to see."

And what a fetching picture she made on the quilt, naked, smiling, and rosy.

"I don't want sex at all. I want Liam Cromarty's lovemaking."

He came down over her on all fours. "Then you shall have it."

The conversation turned tactile, as Louise mapped him with a sure, firm touch. She listened with her hands, stroking down his sides, kneading his bum, tangling her fingers in his hair.

Liam was retaliating with slow, lazy kisses, when Louise turned her head. "Cromarty, you are the most infernally, maddeningly—you're not one of those men who gets turned on by begging, are you? I draw the line—"

Liam eased down onto his forearms and gave her some of his weight. "Louise, you say where and how. I say when. Can we agree on that much?"

"If when is soon."

"Compared to two years, twenty minutes is not—"

"Two *years*, Liam? Oh, honey, I'm so sorry."

Liam kissed her brow. When she called him *honey* in that tone of voice, he was helpless not to kiss some part of her.

"You ought to be pleased not to find yourself on the worktable in the studio," Liam growled, "mud everywhere and a forgotten stylus digging into your tender parts."

"I'd be more pleased if you'd—"

"Spare me from a determined woman." Artists were like this. They fixed on an idea, and had to harp and refine and focus on it until they'd badgered the notion into complete submission.

Liam grabbed his sporran off the night table, found a condom, and put it on. "Are you happy now, Miss Cameron?"

She studied his rampant cock more closely than she had any of the Old Masters at the portrait gallery.

"I'm about to be very happy, Mr. Cromarty."

Liam granted himself a moment to gather his thoughts, to breathe, to take stock, and *be present*. This felt right, felt like moving forward, like trusting in life again.

He positioned himself against Louise, then laced their fingers against the pillow. "Hold on, and tell me if I'm gettin' it wrong."

Louise closed her fingers around his. "Same goes, Cromarty. Hold on, and tell me if I'm getting it wrong."

They got it *right*. Liam joined them slowly, pausing to savor and kiss, and breathe together, to nuzzle and rejoice. Louise matched his rhythm beautifully, untangling one hand to anchor on his bum, her ankles locked at the small of his back. The sheer pleasure of her eagerness, the glory of her sweet heat, the sense of shared desire swamped Liam's entire awareness.

He sent his mind in search of words. "Say when, Louise."

"Liam."

He took that for a *when* and picked up the tempo to slow, hard lunges. Louise clutched at him with gratifying desperation and *when* became *now*, and then, for a moment, *forever*. Pleasure cascaded up through Liam, bringing light, joy, and a sense of well-being so profound he could have wept.

And laughed, and laughed, and laughed.

When he'd stopped heaving like a racehorse, he settled for a smiling kiss to Louise's ear. "God bless America."

She chortled, her belly bouncing against his. "Now look what you've done."

He'd slipped from her body, though the way she patted his backside won her a place in his heart. Gentle, firm, proprietary, protective, and bit scolding.

"No worries," he said, heaving to his hands and knees. "I've another frenchie in my sporran."

She brushed his hair back. "A french—oh. We have other names for them. Only one?"

Lovely woman. "You'll find more in the drawer, but we'll have to replace those. Jeannie would notice."

Louise began carefully unrolling the condom from Liam's softening cock. "At least she doesn't go through the trash."

Morag might. Liam made a mental note to take the trash to his house. "I could have done that, Miss Cameron."

"I'll let you get it the next three times," Louise said. "For now, I need a cuddle."

Liam's tushy was sufficiently adorable that Louise tried to memorize its contours as he moved from the bed to the bathroom. He left the door open, so she could watch him standing at the sink, washing his hands, then rubbing at himself with a damp washcloth.

He was a man in his prime, gloriously healthy, and an inspiration to anybody with a visual/spatial imagination.

"I want to sketch you," Louise called.

"First you want to cuddle, then you want to sketch," he groused, drying his hands. "Next I suppose you'll be raiding my sporran for a bite of tablet. Fickle is woman."

"You brought me tablet?" Thoughtful of him.

"I usually have some with me, and you seem to enjoy it."

Liam was no boy, and thus he had wounds and scars, parts of himself he kept guarded. Louise would not ask if he always had condoms in that sporran, because he'd already told her—

"Did you check the date on those French whatevers?" she asked as he climbed back into bed.

"I bought them last night," he said. "Had to buy more cat food and grabbed them on the same trip."

Louise wrestled Liam against her side, or pushed and

tugged until he figured out where she wanted him.

"You're a friendly sort," Liam remarked, his cheek resting on the slope of her breast. "Though a simple, 'Liam, may I hold you?' might get the job done faster."

*Liam, may I fall in love with you?* Louise would scare him off if she asked that, and she'd scared herself by even thinking it. They lived on opposite sides of an ocean, for criminy sakes.

She traced the contour of his ear, a more complicated appendage than most people realized—on many levels.

"Liam, may I interrogate you?"

He heaved a seismic male sigh. "I married while I was at uni, her name was Karen. She thought I had ambition, I thought she had a nice laugh. She was an accountant, though she also enjoyed cooking."

Louise waited, because these were the introductory recitations, the ones that not only didn't hurt, they comforted a little.

"We married," Liam said, "and then, I fell in love. With Caravaggio, with Vermeer, with Canaletto, the Venus of Willendorf, the Lascaux cave paintings, Fabergé eggs, and early medieval manuscripts. With all things beautiful and profound and interesting. What my wife thought was ambition was merely passion. I didn't figure that out until it was too late."

Louise stroked her fingers through his hair. "You haven't told this story to anybody, have you?"

"My family knows some of it. That feels good."

So, no. He'd carried these regrets and memories around for years rather than entrust them to another.

"I'll tell you a story when you're through," Louise said. Liam wouldn't laugh at her, wouldn't tell her to stop overreacting and feeling sorry for herself.

He kissed her shoulder. "I'll listen, and there isn't much more to tell of mine. I wrote some articles, comparing porcelain to cave paintings, Vermeer to Warhol. I was too inexperienced and cocky to understand that wasn't the done thing. The galleries loved those articles, the academicians didn't know what to do with them, and in short order, I was Dr. Liam Cromarty, PhD, attending the openings, speaking at the conferences."

"You're not telling me all of it. You got into some pissing contest with another hotshot, you failed to spot a forgery, you stepped in doo-doo somehow."

Liam might be the expert on Vermeer's influence on Fabergé, but Louise had four PhD's in how to step in doo-doo.

"I'm not sure what a pissing contest is," he said, "but suffice it to say, I was so busy racking up frequent-flier miles and being witty and insightful at gallery openings, I lost track of my wife."

"Was she ill?"

Liam wasn't ill, but he was ailing, with regret, with old grief, and with the loneliness those burdens caused. Louise could feel them in him the way she could feel cold at the center of a ball of clay.

"Karen was not ill. She was sick of me, and my silly little academic self-importance. I was growing tired of it myself, tired of being the infallible expert on everything, and the one expected to debunk popular theories and pass judgment on all the new talent."

The bedroom felt cozy rather than gloomy, though the rain was coming down in earnest. Dougie strolled into the room and hopped up on the bed, settling in along Louise's other side.

*Good kitty.*

"The new talent never ends," Louise said. She'd been new talent once, to the extent the small world of ceramic art had new talent. "And most new talent shouldn't quit the day job no matter how good they are or what the work is selling for."

"I should have stayed home," Liam said, reaching across Louise to pet the cat. "I should have taught my classes and given my wife the children she wanted. When we married, we agreed children were not a priority, and Karen didn't bring it up until I'd finished my doctorate and landed the teaching post. And then…"

The cat's purr added a comforting touch to the gathering.

"Then?" Louise prompted.

"Then she brought up children again. We argued, we made up, we argued again. I wasn't ready, she wasn't getting any younger. We separated off and on for two years. She said the ambition she'd so admired in me had become selfishness and a thousand other faults, and of course, when that's the reception a man gets, he finds reasons to present papers at conferences all over the globe."

The rain gusted, a spatter of droplets rattling against the skylight. Louise fished around in the Magic Man Purse and found the bag of tablet.

"Have one," she said, holding a cube up to Liam's lips. He nibbled obediently. When she kissed him, the flavor lingered, though so did his regret.

"We were separated," he said, softly. "The longest separation so far, and I had made up my mind that if it would make her happy, we'd try for a baby. I loved her, she was my wife, the rest of it—the gallery openings, the keynote speeches, the growing list of publications—they weren't making me happy. They'd made her miserable, and that was no reflection on me or the vows I'd taken."

This would have been easier to hear if Liam had cheated with any woman besides the squat little Venus of Willendorf, if he'd asked for a divorce, if he'd done anything but turn up decent when it really counted.

Louise drew the covers around his shoulders. "Tell me the rest of it."

"We agreed to spend the weekend together at the same cottage where we'd honeymooned. The plan was to talk. I thought I'd come up with the surefire scheme to save the marriage and recover a bit of my self-respect. I'm not sure what Karen had in mind. She listened, she cried, she told me she loved me. Then as we walked around the loch, she collapsed. By the time I'd carried her back to the cottage, she was gone."

"Heart attack? Stroke?" What other sudden death claimed an otherwise healthy young woman?

"Ectopic pregnancy, and before you ask, no. The child could not have been mine."

*Well, hell.* "This is the bad breakup you mentioned?" The worst breakup imaginable, for what woman conceives another man's child when she's intent on salvaging her marriage?

"Aye. I was so bewildered, and angry and guilty. There's most of a year I can't recall and probably wouldn't want to. I turned mean and condescending, to my colleagues, to my students, to my family. Heavy drinking turned into stupid drinking."

He fell silent for a moment, maybe sorting between bad memories, awful memories, and periods of no memory at all.

"If I'd been a dog," he went on, "somebody would have shot me out of simple kindness, but I was the *brilliant young scholar* who hadn't the sense to do his grieving in private. I had keynote speeches to give on important topics such as romantic elements in post-modern commercial art."

Louise blinked, hard, because tears would not help. They wouldn't help a wife who'd hit the end of her rope. They wouldn't help Liam. They wouldn't help anybody.

"I'm sorry, Liam. I'm so very, very sorry. For you, for her. No wonder you went into a tailspin." Louise pushed him to his back and climbed over him, blanketing him with her body. "Does your family know?"

"Jeannie or Morag might suspect the baby wasn't mine. My younger brothers were certainly concerned. They were all friends with Karen, of a sort. They've never said, and I haven't asked."

Liam was beyond tears, which was sad in itself, but also a

relief. Louise would have lost it if he'd been able to cry.

"Who was the father?"

"What does that matter? I failed my wife, left her to loneliness and frustration, and the one thing she asked of me, I denied her. I suspect she was involved with one of the fellows from the art history department, a quiet man who listens well but doesn't publish much."

Louise sat up and brushed Liam's hair away from his brow. His gaze held sadness, but also resignation, and that…that was wrong.

"Liam Cromarty, you are entitled to your grief, to your bad year, to your tailspins and bad days, and regrets. But you've punished yourself long enough, and you'll listen to what I have to say now."

"Listen to this email," Dunstan Cromarty said to his wife as he joined her on the sofa near the wood stove. "It's from Liam, and he may finally have finished going daft: 'Chauffering your spinster lawyer friend about for the next two weeks as a favor to Jeannie. Miss Cameron likes tablet. Dougie likes her. What do we know about her, other than that she's a Cameron? Love to Jane, Liam.'"

Jane pushed an indignant Wallace off her lap and curled up against her husband.

"If your cousin thinks Louise is a spinster, he's a few drams short of a bottle, Dunstant. At least he e-mailed you."

While Louise had yet to e-mail Jane. Wallace hopped back up and appropriated Dunstan's lap. Atop the piano across the room, Blackstone was busy at his bath.

"I think Liam means the word spinster as a compliment," Dunstan said, scratching the back of Wallace's neck. "Liam is a spinster too."

A mighty handsome one, though Liam was also shy, and married to his job. "How long ago did his wife die?" Jane asked.

"Nearly five years. Liam and Karen were having a rough patch, and he did not cope well. I almost moved home, but my practice was finally starting to take hold. Do you think Louise will come back to the practice of law? She's damned good."

Jane could *feel* Wallace purring, though he did so quietly. She purred when Dunstan petted her too.

"Louise was damned miserable, Dunstan. She's not... Louise has no mean streak, no competitive edge. One of her art professors stole a glazing process she'd developed as an undergrad. She'd been working on it for years, since high school, and he was her adviser. I suspect he was also wooing her, and when he took credit for her work, she just slunk off to law school."

"Don't the senior academic types often take credit for the work their students do?" Dunstan gently unhooked Wallace's front claws from his jeans. "This cat is determined to draw blood."

Wallace had become more territorial since Blackstone had joined the household, though Blackstone was like his owner: very pretty, very self-contained, never imposing, never asking anything of anybody.

"Louise should have raised a stink," Jane said. "Her pottery takes your breath away, and it's simply pottery. This Hellenbore guy was some big deal at the art school, and Louise found out he'd done the same thing five years earlier with another female student's use of mixed media."

Dunstan wrapped an arm across Jane's shoulders. "I don't know what mixed media is, but Louise's cross-examination has taken more than one judge's breath away. You could call her, let her know the family's been fretting over Liam for years."

And make it obvious that Jane was fretting over Louise?

"What then, Dunstan? A half-dozen guys went gaga over Louise in law school, and I think most of the State's Attorney's Office of either gender would love to ask her out. She couldn't be bothered with any of them. Once bitten, twice shy."

"I rather like it when you nibble on me," Dunstan murmured, shifting the cat to the floor. "And I adore nibbling on you."

He demonstrated his adoration on Jane's shoulder, while Jane tried to hold on to her train of thought.

"What if Louise takes a bite out of Liam?" she asked. "Loves him and leaves him? She could do that—no chance of things getting messy if you're packing a round-trip ticket."

Which Jane had insisted on—like an idiot. .

The cat hopped up again and marched across Jane to resume his place on Dunstan's lap.

"Jane, my dearest love, I'm every bit as worried Liam will avail himself of Louise's charms and then wave her on his way. Jeannie says for a year or so, he occasionally dallied, but never gave his heart away, and then he stopped even dallying. This e-mail is not from a man smitten by true love."

"They're adults," Jane said, scratching the cat's chin, which provoked more soft rumbling. "They'll sort it out."

Dunstan was quiet for a moment. He wasn't a loud husband. He was a hardworking and calm husband—also cunning.

"What are you thinking, Dunstan Cromarty?"

"I'll tell Liam if he hurts Louise, you'll kill him."

Well, that was honest. "And if Louise hurts him?"

"You'll have to kill her, my dear. I'll be too busy worrying about my cousin."

Louise Cameron in a stern mood—when naked—was an imposing, alluring sight. Liam's mind filled with images of Nike, goddess of victory, fierce and lovely, both.

"I'm listening, Louise."

"Karen could have fought for you."

Liam resisted the urge to get his mouth on Louise's nipples, which were one shade darker than her lips. That color, a delicate, rococo blend of pink, cream, and—old gold, maybe?—would forever after be *"Louise"* to him.

And the daft woman wanted to lecture him. "Karen and I fought. I didn't enjoy it."

"She probably didn't either, but I'm saying she could have fought *for* you."

"Come here," Liam said, urging Louise down to his chest. "I'm a visual thinker, you see, and my concentration isn't up to the strain presented by your many charms."

He'd made her laugh, which led him to hope she'd leave off nattering about Kar—

"She was your wife, Liam. Did she ever read the papers you wrote?"

Liam traced his way, bump by bump, down Louise's spine. "She wasn't an art historian." As a young husband, he'd been baffled by what seemed to him an indifference to beauty. Karen hadn't been indifferent to beauty. She'd been indifferent to Liam's passion for it.

"Anybody should be able to grasp the substance of whatever you wrote for the galleries or general readership magazines."

"I suppose." Liam had written enough of those articles. Pointless, all of them.

"Did Karen ever join you for a conference?"

"What would she have done at a portraiture conference, or a conference on Dutch Renaissance masters?"

"Liam, if I took you to Amsterdam for a long weekend at a legal conference, you'd find a way to entertain yourself. Same with New York, San Francisco, Rome. Even an accountant has leave, and you had frequent-flier miles."

Liam's sense of well-being ebbed, leaving his old friends weariness and bewilderment in its place. Louise made the same arguments Liam had made—for the last two interminable years of his marriage.

*Come with me, please. To the opening, to the conference, to the reception.*

"She could have gone to counseling with you," Louise

went on. "She could have suggested a second honeymoon, audited one of your courses. She could have waited. She could have done foster care for older children. When people come to me for a divorce, they've often been struggling for ten years, in and out of counseling, changing jobs so they commute less or make more, trying a different neighborhood, or taking ballroom dance classes. They try *anything*, and they fight for their marriages. Karen whined for a couple years about a baby when she knew children weren't a priority for you."

Liam wanted to stuff his head under the pillow, except a small, exhausted, battle-weary part of him refused to hide from Louise's logic.

*We shouldn't speak ill of the dead.*

*Karen's not here to defend herself.*

*I neglected my wife.*

*I should have tried harder.*

The accusations of his conscience, all served up with a dram or three of whisky, which was perhaps the local equivalent of serving pecan pie to a girl struggling with her weight.

Liam wasn't angry at Karen for dying. He was angry at her for taking a piece of his soul with her—*and he had been angry long enough.*

"You are so fierce, Louise Cameron," he said, cradling her jaw between his hands. "Enough talk, enough dwelling on the past. We're alive, and there's no place I'd rather be, nobody I'd rather be with, nothing I'd rather be doing. Make love with me."

The words were a spell, an incantation, that brought a quiet *joie de vivre* trickling back through him.

And they were the truth. Liam leaned up and kissed Louise, not politely or tenderly, but like a man starved for her ferocity and ready to shower his own upon her.

The cat leaped off the bed, Louise laughed, and then she kissed the hell out of Liam while she fished on the night table for his sporran.

# CHAPTER FIVE

Louise saved Culloden Battlefield for a sunny, mild day. The site of a battle that had cost a nation its hopes of holding the British throne, and much, much more, was sobering even in spring sunshine. Liam was quiet as they walked the paths over the moor.

"This place is lovely," Louise said, "and that feels... both wrong and right."

"Wrong that they should have died amid such beauty, right that they should rest here," Liam said. "Shall we sit?"

Any Scot would be sobered by a visit to Culloden, where Scot had fought against Scot by the thousands, and post-battle retaliation by the Crown had been so harsh as to become a foundational component of the national psyche.

"Is there a silver lining?" Louise asked, taking Liam's hand. "The land is still a boggy moor, but did any good come of this?"

Had the American Civil War produced any silver linings? Did any war?

"The clans haven't massacred each other since," Liam said. "But then, after Culloden, the clans were all but obliterated in a political sense. May I change the subject?"

An older couple strolled by, hand in hand, accompanied by a terrier in a Royal Stewart plaid jacket who sniffed the grass beside the path, then trotted ahead.

"Of course you can change the subject," Louise said, because her time in Scotland had dwindled to days, and they'd yet to talk about what came next.

*If anything.* Twice Louise had been ready to have that conversation, and twice Liam's phone had rung at the exact wrong moment. He'd taken the calls, business of some sort, and Louise had wandered off to nibble tablet or admire the infinite shades of green that were Scotland in spring.

Liam kissed her knuckles, one of the countless small gestures of affection with which he was so generous.

"What I'd like to ask you is this: You told me last week that Karen could have fought for me rather than with me," he said. "Is there somebody who should have fought for you?"

A man who saw aesthetic parallels between stone fertility figures and Georgian portraiture would make that leap, and abruptly, the bleak battlefield was the perfect location for what needed to be said.

"Yes, Liam. Somebody should have fought for me, and instead threw down their weapons without firing a shot. When I was finishing up at art school, the champion who failed to join battle was *me*. I knuckled under, to Aunt Ev, to pecan pie, to common sense."

Fighting had never occurred to Louise, not against her family, not against Hellenbore, not against her own broken heart.

"I'm sorry," Liam said. "When we're young, we're reckless about wading into a fight, but often for the wrong causes. Is there a way to make it right?"

Interesting question. The terrier went yapping off into the treacherous, swampy ground that had been the end of so many hopes nearly three hundred years ago. When the old man whistled, the dog came loping back to him.

"How do you make something like that right?" Louise murmured, letting her head rest on Liam's shoulder. "I was lied to, my work misrepresented, and my future knocked on its ass. I knew I had talent, and yet all I did was go home to my parents, and apply to law school."

"You're making it right every time you sit at your wheel," Liam said. "Atonement can take time."

He spoke from experience, and his tale wanted telling, so Louise held back the details of her own regrets.

"Before Karen died—I can say those words now, and they only ache, they don't decimate—before Karen died, when I was racketing about, holding forth on three continents about some damned sculpture or kylix, I was befriended by several of the New York critics."

That bunch. Most critics lacked the gift of creation, so many of them turned to destruction instead. Boggy ground, indeed.

"This doesn't end well," Louise said. If she and Liam had been in bed—Liam slept at the cottage now—she would have climbed on top of him and held on tight.

"It ends," he said, his arm coming around Louise's shoulders. "Sometimes, that's the best we can do. One older fellow chatted me up at every opportunity, always bringing up the latest collections, the latest first shows, the latest articles. I never suspected he was using my half-pickled insights, my off-the-cuff opinions, to recycle into his blog posts. He was clever with words, but his grasp of art sadly wanting, and he was unkind."

Someone had figuratively stolen Liam's glazes. Amazing, how angry Louise was on his behalf, while for herself she'd been simply hurt and ashamed.

Amazing too, the comfort she took from Liam's hand in hers, and his arm around her shoulders.

"You put the bullets into the gun he fired at others' hopes and creativity, Liam, but he fired the gun, not you."

"If I'd had any aspirations toward art criticism, that experience put me off them permanently. Some of the damage he did others haunted me for years, though I took what steps I could to make things right. The advantage he took of my carelessness helped me put aside the hard liquor."

The old couple had walked around nearly the entire battlefield now, their pace measured, though they moved as one unit.

"I want to capture this," Louise said. "I want that couple, their enduring connection, and the way it blesses even this place. I want a wheel where I can throw the love and the sorrow, both, and finish it with a hundred colors nobody has seen before. I'm not going back into that law office, Liam. I know that now."

He kissed her cheek, on that bleak, sunny bench, and Liam Cromarty could say volumes with his kisses. *I'm proud of you. I'm glad for you. You'll do it. Your dreams are worthy. You deserve to be happy.*

But was he saying *I love you?*

Louise loved Liam. Loved how with him she could talk about anything or simply be silent with him.

"You never finished your own story, Louise," he said, tugging her to her feet. "The one about art school, and not standing up for yourself. If you thought law school was a place to lick your wounds, then you were at a sorry pass."

They wandered along in the same direction as the older couple, who'd apparently made their circuit and gone back into the battlefield museum.

"I didn't need to *feel* in law school, Liam. I only needed to think, get enough sleep, and get the assignments done. With my senior art school project, I fell afoul of one or those critics. My adviser claimed any critical notice was good for aspiring artists, so when the great and powerful Stephen Saxe brought his minions on a tour of the campus gallery, the entire senior class was nearly drunk with anxiety."

In the middle of the battlefield, Liam stopped and put his arms around Louise. He said nothing, so she fortified herself with his affection.

"Saxe went after my showing," she said, "tore it to shreds, said it was well executed but at best a slavish tribute to the new glazing technique my adviser had debuted the previous weekend at his show downtown. If after four years of study at the knee of a master, all I could do was derivative work, then maybe my degree should be in Teacher's Pet, not art."

Louise waited for Liam to say something, to console, to philosophize, to heap scorn on the head of the critic who'd be so cruel to a mere student, or the professor who'd steal credit for her creative accomplishment.

"I knew Saxe," Liam said, eventually. "I learned to avoid him. I'm so very sorry, Louise." For a progression of moments, bathed in sunshine and spring breezes, he simply held her while she gathered her courage.

"Hellenbore stole my process," she said, the first time she'd spoken those words out loud to somebody who might grasp their full import. "He set up his own show, and I'm nearly certain he arranged for Saxe to make that royal progress to a mere student exhibition for the express purpose of wrecking my career before I had a career. I never saw it coming, but that experience taught me to anticipate the ambushes even in the courtroom, and never threaten with a figuratively empty gun."

Liam knew the art world, was part of it, and should have been one person to whom Louise could confide this story and earn some commiseration.

He dropped his arms, took her hand, and resumed walking. "Guns are dangerous to all in their ambit, Louise. I can see why you'd not enjoy the legal profession."

The comment was... off. Not the Liam she knew and wanted desperately to love. Scotland's outlook on guns wasn't the same as what Louise had grown up with, but Liam wasn't talking about firearms.

"I never figured out how to bring suit against Hellenbore," Louise said, "or how to get even with Saxe, but I became good at being a lawyer, up to a point. The law is the law and the rules are the rules, but the rules can go only so far toward solving the problems we create with each other. That drove me crazy."

"Maybe it drove you un-crazy," Liam said, passing her a piece of tablet. "You've found your art again, or you soon will."

Louise took a bite and gave Liam back the rest. Next would come the shared bottle of water, or perhaps they'd stop in the museum's snack shop for soup, bread, and butter.

A few days in a borrowed studio wasn't finding her art again, though those days had been lovely.

"Did you stop eating meat when Karen died?"

"Aye."

"Because she was a good cook, and the kitchen smells reminded you of her?"

"You're very astute. I didn't figure it out so quickly, but by then I was out of the carnivore habit. Shall I take a picture of you?"

This place had put Liam's mood off. He was present and he was dodging into shadows, much like the man who'd met her at the airport.

"I want a picture of us, Liam."

"I'm not very photogenic, how about if I—" He got his phone out of his sporran. "I'll take you and you take me?"

He was the most photogenic man Louise had ever met, and this prevarication wasn't like him.

"Not good enough, Cromarty. I know Culloden is a sad place, but I'm happy to be here with you." Louise flagged down a couple chatting in German and gestured and smiled them into taking a photo of her and Liam against the stone cairn at the center of the battle field.

The image was well composed and well exposed, though Liam's smile was pained, his eyes bleak.

"Shall I send you a copy?" Louise asked.

Liam peered at the screen of her phone, coming close enough to put a hint of woodland and heather on the morning breeze.

"We'll do better elsewhere, I think. Are you thirsty?"

"Sure." Louise swilled from the bottle of Highland Spring, then passed it to Liam when she wanted to throw her arms around him.

Even to tell him she loved him, though this sad morning on a battlefield wasn't the time or place.

"C'mon," she said, taking his hand. "Let's blow this popsicle stand and head down to Cairngorms National Park. They have reindeer there, don't they? We don't have reindeer in Georgia, and if we did, we'd probably hunt them to extinction."

— ❧ —

Liam had bought a damned ring yesterday, while Louise had been engrossed in her wheel. An emerald stone, more valuable than diamonds and appropriate for Louise's fire and sense of purpose. The setting was Celtic gold, and the sentiments…

Louise had put the heart back in him, and Liam didn't want her to leave, ever.

Though now, the sooner he put her on that plane, the better for them both.

As Louise boiled up a batch of gnocchi, Liam opened the wine and prepared to lie his way through the rest of Louise's visit.

"Will you throw tonight?" he asked. Louise could work at her wheel for hours, and he had the sense she was only warming up. Five years' penance for another's crimes rode her hard, and she'd throw her way free of it.

"Nah. No throwing tonight. Tromping around all day wore me out. If you'll slice the bread, I'll set the table."

At every meal Liam ate with his family, every single meal, somebody had to make a joke about his decision to stop eating meat. Louise hadn't remarked on it once. When they planned meals, her suggestions were meatless, and she was the next thing to a cheese connoisseur.

They'd toured a distillery in Inverness, and she'd made the most awful face at one of the world's best-loved Highland single malts.

*Of course*, Liam had bought her a ring, and fool that he was, returning it would about kill him. He'd been about killed before and didn't care to repeat the experience.

"Shall I dress the salad?" Louise asked.

"Please, and I'll pour."

Louise chose the wines, because Louise chose the cheeses. Main dishes were Liam's province, and salads and dessert were negotiated.

Though what in God's name would they talk about now?

*Say, Louise, did you know that Saxe's insults to your work weren't even original? I sneered and snickered my way past all those lovely vases, those intriguing drinking cups, and the teapot that shed rainbows in all directions, though even I admitted a student's derivative work was superior to what Hellenbore had displayed a week earlier.*

Saxe had left that part out, of course. Liam took a sip of wine, but just a sip. He'd earned this misery, and by God, he'd endure it.

Though not alone. Before conversation could turn awkward or intimate, Uncle Donald came clomping onto the porch.

"I smell dinner," he said, setting his tackle down outside the front door. "Don't suppose there's room for a lonely old man at the table?"

"A shameless man in his prime," Louise said, joining Liam at the door. "The boots can stay out here, though, and you will wash your hands."

"I like her," Donald said, toeing off a pair of green Wellies. "Has a confident air and a nice behind."

"No dessert for you, auld man," Louise said over her shoulder. "We're politically correct at Dunroamin Cottage, if we know what's good for us."

For once, Liam was affirmatively glad to see his uncle, who could tell story after story, about everything from the Battle of the Shirts to Mary Queen of Scots, to epic rounds of golf at St. Andrews.

When the meal had been consumed, the coffee and tablet had made the rounds, and Donald had told stories on half the Cromarty clan, he kissed Louise's cheek and rose.

"I'll be off then. Shall I feed your puppy, Liam?"

"You have *a puppy*?" Louise asked.

"He has an old blind dog," Donald said. "Or half-blind. She's good company fishing, is Helen."

"Helen's getting on," Liam said, taking his dishes to the sink. "She's not blind in the least, but she is good company if you're inclined to stay in one spot for hours."

"If you like spending time with bears," Donald said, snitching another piece of tablet. "Louise strikes me as the better bargain."

Louise rose and shoved the mostly empty wine bottle at him. "Time to go, you. Comparing ladies to dogs is no way to win friends and influence women. Don't forget your fishing pole."

Liam loved hearing Louise talk. Bits of Georgia crept in— fishin' pole, instead of fishing rod, or rod and reel—and her tone was always warm.

"I'll do the dishes if you want to take your shower," he said when Donald had gone stomping on his way, singing about the rashes-o, and drinking from the bottle.

*I don't want to be like that.* Liam didn't want to be old and alone, smelling of river mud, swilling leftover wine, and deriving a sense of usefulness by feeding a dog who barely woke up between meals anymore.

"I'm dead on my feet," Louise said, putting plastic wrap over the salad. "If you're sure you don't mind cleaning up, I'll see you upstairs."

Reprieve. Another forty-five minutes when Liam wouldn't

have to make conversation, wrestle guilt, and count the minutes until Louise's departure. He kissed her cheek and patted her bottom.

"Away with you, then, madam. Dougie and I will manage. Don't wait up for us."

She hugged him—Louise was unstinting with her affection, something Liam would not have guessed about her when he'd fetched her from the airport.

And then she was gone, leaving Liam with a messy kitchen, and more heartache than one tired, lonely Scot should have to bear.

—◦◦◦◦◦—

By Louise's last day at the cottage, an invisible elephant in pink Scottish plaid had joined her vacation entourage. The elephant carried around a load of questions nobody was asking anybody.

*So, what happens after the plane takes off?*
*Will you call me?*
*Will I see you again?*

Liam made endlessly tender, quiet love to her, then came at her with ferocious passion. Then it was Louise's turn to be tender, to memorize the turn of his shoulders, the line of his flanks, the texture of his skin at the small of his back.

She spent hours at the wheel and more hours online doing research—about glazes, collections, art schools, and the past. Hellenbore had retired amid some scandal involving an undergraduate "prone to depression."

"She should be furious, not depressed," Louise informed the drinking cup on the wheel. "But if she forced him into retirement, maybe she should be proud."

The cup spun on the wheel, perfectly symmetric, but plain. No colors, no variations in texture or form to give it life.

"You need to eat," Liam said from the doorway. He watched her from time to time, but he neither asked questions nor asked them lately. The studio hardly had room for Louise's heartache, Liam's quiet presence, and that damned pink elephant.

"I need to finish up," Louise said, dragging the cutoff wire under her clay. "I'll be an hour at least cleaning the knives, scrapers, and other tools. You don't have to help."

Liam's brows twitched. As an older man, he'd have bushy brows. That single twitch confirmed that Louise's elephant was getting restless, putting a sharpness on her words she hadn't intended.

By this time tomorrow, Louise would have left Scotland, possibly forever.

"I can make dinner," Liam said. "I notice you haven't started to pack."

Whatever the hell that meant.

Louise mashed the clay back into a hard, compact ball. "I'm quick when it comes to throwing my things into a suitcase. If we're making pizza, we'll need ingredients. I'll clean up, you make a grocery run, and we'll meet in the kitchen."

"Sounds like a plan."

Liam sauntered over to her, kissed the top of her head, and would have left, except Louise caught his clean hand in her muddy one.

"I'll miss you, Liam. I'll miss you terribly."

Another kiss. "Likewise, Louise Mavis Cameron."

Then he was gone.

Louise dealt with the tools of her trade—her art—and tidied up the studio until it was as clean and welcoming as she'd found it. She grabbed a shower for good measure and was toweling off when another question joined her already overflowing supply.

How had Liam known her middle name? She'd never told him, not specifically, which middle name went with which Cameron sister, and yet he'd known her middle name was Mavis.

Interesting.

Words stuck in Liam's throat all the way to the airport, while beside him, Louise held her peace. A woman who'd been cheated out of her future as an artist by a lot of stupid, arrogant men probably learned to keep her own counsel very well.

"Are you nervous?" Liam asked as they tooled over the Forth Road Bridge.

"I have it on good authority that flying to the States is easier than flying to Europe. What will you do with yourself today, Liam?"

He'd get the cottage ready for Jeannie's next rental, respond to the emails he'd neglected for the past two weeks, and get on with the business of hating himself for the rest of his life—again.

"I'll catch up on the housework, mostly."

They reached the southern bank of the firth, that much closer to the airport.

"Liam, you have a beautiful house. I didn't poke around inside, though when I took Helen back yesterday, I couldn't help but admire it. Somebody went to a lot of trouble with that house, a lot of expensive trouble."

This was a question he could answer. "How do I afford that place on a college professor's salary?"

"You have art everywhere. Nice art."

"That's not only art, that's inventory, Louise. For years, when I saw something I liked, I bought it. Small things at first, then larger pieces. You'd be surprised what major corporations and even law firms are willing to pay for a bit of the pretty for their offices."

Louise left off pretending to be fascinated with the traffic around them. "You're a *dealer*? That's why you get phone calls from all over the world and jabber away in French and German?"

"Not quite a dealer," Liam said. "I don't sell the pieces I own, I rent them out. When a client wants a different look, I find them something else, from what's on hand, in storage, or in various galleries that know what I like. It's rather profitable."

The smile Louise aimed at him was both admiring and knowing. "That's why you don't bring it up with your family? You're embarrassed to make money at something you enjoy?"

Liam would miss Louise for the rest of his life, miss her quickness, her understanding, her passion for cheese, and the way she held entire conversations with a lump of wet clay.

"I simply don't know how to tell them," Liam said. "I make money, the world has a little more good art to enjoy, the businesses are happy, the artists have a paying client and the occasional commission. It doesn't seem fair that I'd also enjoy the work."

The airport was only a few minutes ahead, and yet, what more could Liam say?

*I ruined your career years ago, but don't mind that, because sometime in the past two weeks, I fell in love with you.*

"You'll let Jeannie know when you're home?" he asked.

"Sure. Or I can text you."

"Please do. I'll worry." And probably kick hard objects, yell at the cat, and ignore messages from family. Familiar territory.

After more pained silence, Liam drew up to the departures curb. "I can park if you like."

"No need," Louise said, opening her door. "I've got this, Cromarty, and I want you to know something."

Liam wrestled Louise's colorful suitcase onto the curb and prepared to die right there in the Scottish spring sunshine that had so captivated her two weeks ago.

"I'll miss you, Louise Cameron. I'll miss you sorely."

"I'll miss you, too. Terribly, horribly, awfully, very badly, but here's something to think about, Professor. I spent some time online last night. If I wanted to earn a master of fine arts, some of the best programs in the world are in your backyard.

Some of the most interesting and respected programs, right down the lane in Glasgow."

*What is she saying?*

Louise wrapped Liam in a fierce embrace.

"You'd come back here, to Scotland, Louise?"

"I can throw pots wherever there's a wheel and mud. I can hand-build. I can sketch. I can teach. I can wait tables, muck stalls, or impersonate a lawyer. What I cannot do anymore, ever again, is let my life go by while I wait for happiness to find me. You're right: I need to do what makes me happy, even if I have to fight for it."

Louise kissed his cheek, then stepped back and grabbed the handle of her suitcase. "Thank you, Liam Cromarty. For everything, thank you."

Liam stood staring long after Louise had disappeared into the crowd, until the blare of an insistent horn reminded him that he was holding up traffic. He didn't recall driving back to Perthshire, but he was still pondering Louise's words when he got home and found Uncle Donald dozing in a chair on his front terrace.

"You're an idiot," Donald said, not even opening his eyes.

Liam took a place beside him, sitting right on the hard stones of the terrace. "Aye, and you're where I get it from."

"Lad, you cannot let that one go. Move to America, commute across the ocean, or kidnap her, but don't waste any more time wallowing in your guilt and grief. You'll end up singing to the fish and wondering how seventy-five years can pass in a summer."

Dougie joined the discussion, hopping onto Donald's lap.

"Donald, I've wronged that woman, and I didn't admit it to her. Isn't it better that she recall me as a Highland fling than learn that I played a significant part in her worst betrayals?"

*No, it was not.* Having put Louise on the plane, Liam hated the thought of letting his lies and silence be the last chapter in their story. Could he make it right?

Could he ever make it right?

Helen came panting around the side of the house, wet from the shoulders down and reeking of the river. She shook—of course—baptizing Liam and annoying Dougie too.

"You were a right mess for a bit," Donald said, not uncharitably. "Graduate school and all that whatnot with Karen. That's behind you now. A cat, a smelly dog, and a tipsy old man aren't very good company compared to the lass."

They were good company. Louise was better company.

"Louise makes the most beautiful ceramics you've ever seen, Donald. You did see some of it when I first moved into the house. The perfect blend of shapes, colors, textures… She has magic in her heart."

She still had the magic, maybe more than ever. Liam had felt it vibrating through her when she'd been at her wheel, had gloried in its reflection when they'd made love.

"*Louise* made all those vases and pots and dishes? The blue and the green, and peacocky stuff?"

"When she was only a student. I've rented most of her pieces to a New York law firm that won't send them back to me willingly. That firm represents obscenely successful artists, and her work is exactly what they wanted to grace their common areas. I hadn't connected L. Mavis Cameron with my Louise Cameron."

"Well, then," Donald said, passing Liam the cat and rising. "You have matters to see to, Liam. You'd best get on with them."

Dougie bopped Liam's chin, seconding the motion, apparently.

"Classes start back up in a week, Donald, and Louise wasn't exactly reluctant to get on that plane." Because she was off in search of happiness, and what woman wouldn't relish such a quest?

Donald stopped halfway across the terrace to pet Helen's shaggy head. "Sooner begun is sooner done, Liam Donald

Cromarty. That woman made you happy, and I'd about given up on you."

Liam had about given up on himself. "You think I should fight for her." So did Liam.

"You're not the brightest of my nephews, but you usually come to the right answer eventually. Am I wrong, Liam?"

Liam rose, the cat in his arms. For two weeks, he'd had somebody to share his meals with, also his bed, and his heart. Those two weeks had been the best he could recall.

"I'm saying you're right, Uncle, but this is a battle I must win, and putting together my strategy will take some time."

"I'll be at the river," Donald said, disappearing down the steps. "If you should take a notion to travel, I'll look in on your beasts."

"You heard him," Liam informed the dog and cat. "I'd best get busy. In New York the day's already half over."

Liam didn't call, he didn't e-mail. He'd replied to the text Louise had sent two weeks ago confirming her safe return to the United States.

"Rejoicing in your safe arrival there, missing you here. Will be in touch. Throw splendid pots until then. Liam Cromarty."

Not, "Love, Liam."

Not, "Yours, Liam."

Not fondly, sincerely, truly yours…

Louise smashed her clay flat again.

"Are you angry at that clay?" Jane set down the carry out Eritrean on the studio's work table. The space was rented, the light entirely artificial, and the wheel grouchy.

"I did better work in Scotland," Louise said. "I can't focus here. What is wrong with me that I'm attracted to men who—"

Louise's phone rang, blaring "Scotland the Brave," about which Jane apparently knew better than to comment.

"My hands are muddy," Louise said. "Would you get that?"

Though in Scotland, it would be barely seven a.m. Would

Liam call that early?

"I'm not getting this," Jane said. "You're letting it ring through. It's Robert."

"And I had no appetite before the phone rang." Robert and his latest scholarly piece of tripe could abuse semicolons on somebody else's watch. Let his Sweet Young Thing help him get published. "I have pots to throw."

"Wash your hands," Jane said, arranging carry-out containers on the work table. "I brought you a heather ale to try. Dunstan likes it for a change of pace."

Louise turned on the tap at the sink and scrubbed at her hands. Did Liam enjoy heather ale? Was he back at his classes? Had he gone fishing with Donald lest his uncle get too lonely?

"Earth to Louise."

"How is Dunstan?" Louise asked, shutting off the tap and taking a whiff of vegetable sambusas Liam would have delighted in. She should have made them for him, with a nice peppery—

"Dunstan is worried about his cousin Liam." Jane said.

Louise slammed the lid of the container shut. If she'd had clay in her hands, she would have thrown it against the wall.

"Do not mess with me, Jane DeLuca Cromarty. I'm PMSing and nursing a broken heart, my muse is playing hard to get, and I'm about to give notice that I won't be teaching in the fall. Is Liam okay?"

Jane set down her unopened bottle of ale, slowly. "You already quit the lawyer day job, Louise. Are you quitting the artist day job, too?"

"Is. Liam. All. Right?"

"Dunstan can't tell. Liam's preoccupied, according to the family grapevine, but not like he was after his wife died. They're not sure what's up, but Uncle Donald's keeping a close eye on him."

"Uncle Donald isn't exactly a good influence." But he was a cagey old guy who knew a thing or two about loneliness.

Louise opened her ale and passed Jane the bottle opener. "I'm tempted to delete Robert's message."

Louise took a sip of fermented grain and Scotland.

"You deleted Robert from your bedroom that's a start," Jane said around a mouthful of spongy, vinegary injera bread.

Did Liam even like Eritrean cuisine?

"Robert was never there much to begin with," Louise said. "For the last six months, nobody was asking and nobody was telling. He claimed he was on writing deadlines. Leave me some bread."

Jane divided the remaining bread in half. "Robert's in New York. If you move up there for the privilege of reminding him to put the seat down until he finds some other female to sponge off of, I will smack you."

Liam had made sure Louise was never at risk for that kind of behavior again.

"I like this ale," Louise said, peering at the label. "Fraoch is the Gaelic word for heather."

"And Liam is the Gaelic word for heartache," Jane retorted. "Dunstan says Liam has left town, and Donald isn't saying where he went."

Maybe to a cottage near a loch in the Highlands, maybe to purchase more art.

"He's not headed here that I know of," Louise said. "He said he'd be in touch, but that might be Scottish for 'don't let the door hit ya where the good Lord split ya.'"

"You can take the woman out of Georgia..." Jane said. "You going back to Scotland?"

The damned phone rang again. "Robert," Louise said, putting the phone in silent mode. "He must have already run off his Sweet Young Thing."

Jane tore off another strip of bread. "Revenge is mine, sayeth the former girlfriend, but you honestly couldn't be bothered, could you?"

"With Robert? I knew better, Jane. Before law school,

when Hellenbore took such an interest in my glazes and was so encouraging, I was an innocent. Robert was… a distraction."

A lousy distraction.

Jane closed one eye and peered down inside her bottle of ale, managing to look both elegant and silly.

"So if Liam called you in the next fifteen minutes and asked you to join him for a Roman holiday, you'd tell him he's had his shot, one and done?"

"If Liam called, we'd talk about where we go from here," Louise said, assuming her little heart didn't go pitty-patting away with her brain at the sight of even his phone number. "I'd take time to think about any decisions, and he'd understand why."

If Liam could fly to Rome, he could fly to DC. If he could call Singapore, he could call Louise.

"You're not eating much, Louise."

Dunstan would inhale any leftovers Jane took back to the office. Louise used the bread to scoop up another mouthful of spicy potatoes.

"I miss him, Jane. I really, really miss him. He's dear, lovely, an adult, hot, thoughtful…."

"And not calling you," Jane said. "Give it time. Dunstan sometimes takes a while to figure things out. We sort through legal cases together in nothing flat, but family stuff always takes longer."

"You're a good friend."

The phone buzzed, knocking against the table.

"Answer the idiot," Jane said, taking a sip of ale.

Louise glanced at the phone, intending to let Robert's pestering go to voice mail for the third time.

Her stomach gave a funny little hop at the digits crowding her screen. "It's Liam."

# CHAPTER SIX

Jane saluted Louise with her bottle of ale. "Give cousin Liam my love, and then read his beads for not calling. Sooner."

"This is Louise." Steady voice, always a good way to start off.

"Liam here."

Two beautiful, Scottish words, and not quite steady. Was that good? "How are you, Liam?" *Where are you? When can I see you again?*

"Exhausted, but I thought I owed you a bit of warning in case you're entertaining."

"Warning about what? And I am entertaining."

A pause, and not because the call was international. "Shall I call back, Louise?"

She glanced at the wall clock. "Give me fifteen minutes, Liam, and Jane says hello."

"Jane? Dunstan's Jane?" The relief in his voice was sweet.

"The very one. We're having lunch, and she sends her love. When I've run her off and charged up my battery for a few minutes, you can call me back."

"I'll do that. Talk soon."

Louise put the phone back on ring and stared at it. "He

called, but."

"But nothing. He called. If you're not going to eat that bread, I will or Dunstan will. I'm off, and I *will* expect a report by close of business, Louise. Liam is family, and Dunstan's worried about him."

In other words, Jane was worried about Louise.

Louise tore off a nibble of bread. "Liam sounded fine, but... focused. He has an agenda." He'd always had an itinerary for their day. She suspected he'd taken an itinerary to bed with them, too, and they always reached their destination.

Several times.

Jane packed up her half of the largely uneaten meal. "When a man calls with an agenda, then his objective is not ditching you, though I can understand why you might want to ditch him."

"Go," Louise said. "I want to listen to what Liam has to say, and not only because his accent is luscious."

Jane left with a hug and a kiss, bustling off to make Damson County dangerous for opposing counsel, and doubtless to make a report to Dunstan.

"If I moved to Scotland," Louise told her silent wheel, "Jane would visit, because Dunstan's folks are there."

Scotland had cast a spell independent of Liam. The light; the sense of an orderly society balanced with a long, tumultuous history; the natural beauty... the tablet.

"Aunt Ev would *not* visit, a definite plus."

The studio had a single comfortable chair, over by the one north-facing window. Louise took her ale there, cracked the window, and sat down to wait for the longest nine minutes since minutes had been invented.

— ⁓⁂⁓ —

Liam had had such hopes for his plan when he'd been in Scotland, but now... He should have called, he should have discussed this with Louise, he should have waited.

He could not wait. He dialed, heart thumping against his

ribs.

"Hello, Liam."

"Has Jane left?" The soul of charm, he would never be. "I mean, how are you, Louise?"

He'd meant: I've missed you, every night, every day, everywhere.

"Jane executed a tactical, if dignified, retreat. I never asked you: Do you like Eritrean food?"

Would an upset woman ask such a thing? Would an *indifferent* woman ask that question?

"I enjoy the vegetarian dishes and particularly the bread. It wants a good ale, though."

"I like you, Liam. I do not like waiting two weeks for you to *be in touch*."

They'd been a busy, fraught two weeks. "In future, I'll call more frequently." He wouldn't overtly promise that. Louise had probably heard plenty of sly, casual promises from men. "I would enjoy the occasional call from you as well, Louise, in case you were wondering."

"I'm wondering," Louise said, the hint of a Southern accent adding nuances to a mere two words.

"About?"

"Aboot? I've missed hearing your voice, Liam. I've wondered how you are, how the classes for the new term are shaping up, and if you're happy."

A hint of reproach with an entire hug's worth of caring. Liam cast around for something witty, sophisticated, and charming to offer in return.

And failed. "I miss everything about you." Pray God the condition was temporary. "Will you meet me in New York this weekend?"

An indrawn breath and then a pause. "New York is not my favorite place."

Well, of course not. Louise had attended art school there, and nobody wanted to revisit the scene of their worst nightmares.

"I have a meeting to attend Friday in the city," Liam said. "We can stay out in Connecticut, the Hudson Valley, wherever you please. I'd really like to see you."

*Fight for us, Louise. Please, I'm begging you, fight for us.* Though if she declined, Liam would simply drive down to Maryland and put his case before her there. New York was important to his plans, but Louise was indispensable to his happiness.

"Cromarty, your technique needs work. You, I want to see. New York, I don't much care for. Next time we do this, it won't be New York."

Relief, sweet and precious, coursed through him. "Next time we do this, we'll follow your itinerary to the letter. Come up Friday afternoon, and we'll go out for dinner. I want to take you somewhere fancy."

"Do you like heather ale?"

"When a Scotsman says he wants to spend a fortune on your meal, you ask about ale?"

"You've never been parsimonious, Professor. Not in any sense. Find us a hotel in the Village, and I'll take the train up from Baltimore. I'll text you the details."

Liam didn't want to break the connection. "Or you could call me, anytime."

"I just might, but for now, I have pots to throw, Liam. Stay out of trouble until I can get my hands on you."

*And mine on you.* "I'll do that. See you Friday, Louise, and thank you."

—◌◌◌—

For Louise, the thrown pot was the canvas, and the finish work—the glazing and texturing, the etched designs, the surface ornamentation—was where she expressed the greater part of her creativity. Shape, contour, heft, and other physical properties of ceramic art all mattered, but appearance made the first and greatest impact for her.

After Liam's call, Louise allowed herself to glaze, fire, and finish a piece for the first time in five years. She was rooting in her shoulder bag for that small vase when she decided to instead grab her cell phone and check e-mail.

She still hadn't dealt with messages Robert had left several days ago.

The train was barreling toward Penn Station, where Liam would meet her, and Louise wasn't about to listen to Robert's messages once she and Liam had connected.

The last two messages were simply, "C'mon Louise, call me," and "This is rude behavior between colleagues, Lou. Pick up, would you?'"

Colleagues? They'd been roommates with a few unimpressive benefits.

The first message was broken up, something about a showing, and Robert would love to be her date for the evening. He was pleased about something.

*Huh?* If Robert said he was pleased for her, and using that eager, conspiratorial tone, then he was pleased for himself.

Delete. Delete. Delete.

The train pulled into the station, a subterranean dungeon of modern engineering and urban efficiency. Louise stepped onto the platform and extended the handle on her rainbow suitcase. New York was a place that moved forward at a dash not a dawdle, and Louise was moving with it.

*Delete Georgia, delete lawyering, delete regrets.* Maybe delete the entire USA except for the occasional visit. Good-bye to all of it; hello, creativity, courage, and happiness. Louise came up the escalator, into the regular chaos of the station, and there, standing motionless in the middle of it all, was Liam.

He'd worn a kilt, the colorful clan tartan he'd worn to climb Arthur's Seat with her. For a moment, Louise simply beheld him, a calm, handsome guy oblivious to the few glances his attire earned.

Louise rolled right up to him, dropped the handle of her suitcase, and threw her arms around him.

"I love you, Liam Cromarty."

His arms came around her, slowly. "I beg your pardon?"

No regrets, no looking back, no waiting around for good fortune to sprinkle some random luck her way.

"I love you, Liam Cromarty. I've enjoyed every moment I've spent in your company, and I'm very glad you're here. I brought you some sambusas."

"Sambusas are good, if they're not too spicy."

His embrace was desperately snug—and dear—while his words were tentative.

"Relax, Cromarty. When I say I love you, I'm stating a fact that makes me happy. I'm not handing out a pass/fail quiz for you to complete. Let's get out of this noise, and out of our clothes."

Liam turned loose of Louise enough to grab the handle of her suitcase, but kept an arm around her shoulders.

"Aye to both. The sooner, the better."

—◦◦◦◦◦—

Louise's lovemaking had changed in only a few weeks, become more passionate and tender, more lyrical and demanding. Her very walk had changed, from a businesslike gait to an open stride that said she knew exactly where she was going.

*She loved him.* If Liam had doubted Louise's words, he could not doubt her actions. As she wrestled Liam over her and wiggled her way beneath him, her smooth, warm curves, and strong hands eased aches in his heart even before they'd tended to other aches.

"You've missed me, then?" Liam asked, kissing her cheek. He could wallow in the simple scent of her.

"Desperately. How about if we screw like bunnies now and save the romantic stuff for later? This is Manhattan. We can have Eritrean delivered with a side of Thai fusion and designer ice cream chaser."

A sure recipe for indigestion.

"We'll compromise," Liam said, angling his head to take a nipple between his teeth. "We'll be romantic bunnies."

Louise retaliated by grabbing his bum in a potter's very firm grasp, and his hair, and kissing him witless while she wrapped her legs around him and muttered about how he'd better have brought her some tablet.

"I brought you tablet," Liam said, levering up onto his elbows. "I've brought you all manner of sweets, including,"—in one hard, sure thrust, he ended their mutual teasing—"this. God, I've missed you."

They went still for a moment, smiling at each other. Liam needed to see that same smile on Louise's face when the evening ended, too. The thought helped him hold back, helped him impersonate a very romantic, hopelessly besotted rabbit who'd do anything for his lady.

Except change their plans for the evening.

Louise was asleep, her head in Liam's lap, when his phone chimed six-thirty. Outside, the ceaseless screech, thump, and horn blasts of traffic had shifted from the day to the evening song of the city, and the sun was taking its light away.

"Wake up, love," Liam whispered, tousling Louise's hair. "Time for bright lights, big city."

Time to risk everything on the hope that they had a future. A better man would have spent the afternoon sightseeing with her, but Liam simply hadn't been able to. Louise had lived in New York for several years. She didn't need another visit to Rockefeller Plaza, not as badly as Liam needed to have her to himself.

Possibly for one last time.

"Sleep," Louise muttered, nuzzling at him. Thank goodness the sheets came between her cheek and his equipment, because she'd already proved her mouth was a powerful weapon against his best intentions.

"No more of your tricks, Louise Cameron. We need sustenance."

"Carryout."

Any other night with her, in any other city, even in this city. "I brought my Highland dress regalia, and by God you'll help me into it."

Her head came up. "The fussy kilt? With the jacket and vest and knee socks?"

"The very one, though I can still stash some tablet in my sporran." A dress sporran, complete with tassels and silver trim.

Liam explained each piece of the full outfit and affixed his *sgian-dubh* to his left calf, because the evening ought to be a hospitable outing. The only other sharp knife in evidence might be the one Louise would take to his heart.

Liam's cell phone had been quiet for once, an encouraging sign.

When he was properly attired in formal Highland dress, Louise shimmied into a dark green silk sheath that was lovely, but not half so intriguing to Liam as her shimmying.

"Down, laddie," he muttered in the direction of his sporran.

"Will you get the hook at the top of my zipper?" Louise asked, turning her back and sweeping her hair off her nape. The engagement ring Liam had brought with him would go wonderfully with her dress—an encouraging omen, surely.

Liam obliged, though fastening the small hook and eye took several tries. "You'll wear your hair down?"

"Not quite, but give me five minutes for some lip gloss and eyeliner, and I'll be ready to go."

Hotel rooms in New York were priced in proportion to their square footage, and Liam had not splurged on a penthouse. Preparing for the evening together had an extra intimacy because of the cozy quarters, and because getting dressed up for a night on the town was another new, shared experience for them.

A vision in green and grace emerged from the bathroom.

The dress made Louise's natural movements shimmer and slide, and she'd done something with her hair—left it cascading over one shoulder, not up, not down. All manner of curving lines, from her hips to her shoulders, to her knees, danced as she moved.

"I don't believe I've ever seen you in heels," Liam said. Inane remark, but it made her smile.

"These are low heels. I can stand around in them all night, but only you would notice a lady's shoes."

The shoes were a seafoamy green and sparkly, like magic slippers. Gold dangled from Louise's earlobes, and a single jade teardrop hung from a gold chain right above her cleavage.

"I wish, for the first time in my life, that I could paint," Liam said. "We'd need a bed in my studio, though."

"If you keep talking like that, we'll never get to the restaurant," Louise replied, Georgia swaying through her vowels. She picked up a gold clutch purse from the night table and the vision of luscious, relaxed sophistication was complete.

Seven fifteen on the nose. "I've reservations at eight," Liam said, not exactly a lie. "Not far from here, in fact."

"Then lay on, Cromarty, because somebody helped me work up an appetite."

Liam was the envy of every man who saw them, and he'd never had such quick luck hailing a New York cab. As he handed Louise in, and gave the cabby directions, Liam prayed his luck would hold for the rest of the night.

—⁓☙⁓—

A student could live in New York for several years and not learn much more of the town than the nearest cheap restaurants, a couple of suds-yer-duds, and a half-dozen coffee shops. Louise had fared a little better than that, but not much.

"Is this restaurant one of your favorites?" Louise asked as Liam handed her out of the cab.

"I hope you'll like this place," Liam said, winging his arm

at her, though nobody walked down the street in New York arm in arm.

What did that matter? Louise took Liam's arm, though they were in the skyscraper canyons of the Financial District. By day, all would be sunlight reflecting off of new construction, and bustling crowds of sharply-dressed professionals exuding stress and self-importance in equal measure.

"In here," Liam said, gesturing to a discrete, formal façade in the middle of a block. A limousine waited by the curb.

Maybe the restaurant was in the basement or on the roof?

Louise walked with Liam past a reception area where a guard at a desk asked for their names. Louise was too busy studying the frescoes and paintings on the walls to pay much attention.

"This place is gorgeous," she said, when Liam would have hauled her over to the elevators. "Can you imagine what that stained glass looks like in daylight?"

"It's magnificent," Liam said, "and the patterns the window glass makes on the floor on a sunny afternoon are intended to dance with the inlays on the tiles. We'll come back and admire it someday."

A note in his voice caught Louise's attention. They'd have a someday, a lot of somedays, of that Louise was increasingly certain. She didn't need pretty words when she had that steady, tender regard in Liam's blue eyes.

"Let's go to dinner," she said, taking Liam's hand. "We'll do the Met tomorrow, assuming I let you out of bed."

"We'll do the Met," Liam answered, kissing her on the mouth. "Or whatever you please."

He was dangerously good-looking in his finery, not simply because he was a handsome guy. He knew *how* to wear Highland formal attire, knew exactly where the sporran ought to rest, knew the feel of the kilt draped against his thighs.

"I still want to sketch you," Louise murmured as they stepped off the elevator. "Without your clothes, Liam."

They were in another lobby of sorts, a mezzanine space that stretched for much of the floor. People milled about here, and to one side of the area, a buffet had been set up.

The flowers along the buffet were gorgeous without being too showy. Purples and greens with the occasional dash of yellow or red.

"Liam? This does not look like a restaurant." It looked like a reception… or a *showing*. Louise's gaze returned to the flowers, beautiful, understated and vaguely disquieting.

"There's plenty to eat," Liam said. "I made sure of that, and the bar's in that corner. Let's have a look at the main attraction, though, shall we?"

Restaurants did not have main attractions. One of Louise's former professors, a woman who'd done quite well with textiles, waggled her fingers at Louise and disquiet threatened to coalesce into anxiety.

"Robert's here," Louise said, her middle abruptly recalling the bleak feel of Culloden Battlefield. "I never wanted to see him again, Liam. Why would you ask me to get all dressed up just so you could take me someplace where I'd have to deal with *him*?"

And God help her, Larry O'Connor, the grand old man of studio art reviews was over at the bar.

"Robert has come to practice his skills as a hanger-on," Liam said. "The show is public, so I couldn't keep him out even after what Jane had to say about him when I interrogated her yesterday. You needn't speak to him, but you might enjoy his groveling."

Through a set of glass and chrome double doors, somebody moved and Louise caught a flash of a tall vase on a white stand. All manner of blues and greens blended and swirled in the glazes, gold lurked at the edge of every color, and light seemed to pour from the surface.

*"Liam Cromarty, what have you done?"*

O'Connor waved, a jovial little troll of a man who'd spoken

to Louise's classes about art criticism throughout history.

"I have put right a wrong I did nearly a decade ago," Liam said.

His hold on Louise's hand was all that kept her from bolting for the elevators.

"You're not an art critic," Louise said, her heart feeling the pull of the blue and green vase, and whatever else might be behind those double doors. "You have nothing to do with why I went to law school."

"I had everything to do with it, Louise. I was among those Saxe hauled to your showing, to sneer at and ridicule student works, some of which were brilliant. The phrase 'major in Teacher's Pet' originated with me, as did other disparaging remarks. Even as I uttered them, I was baffled at how a student, an undergraduate struggling to emulate her more experienced teacher, could so thoroughly surpass his results."

Liam had both hands wrapped around Louise's fingers. "Then the next morning, I saw my own words in print," he went on, "casual, snide, half-drunken comments meant only for a small, snide, half-drunken group. That day was a turning point for me, the lowest point in a long, stupid fall from decency and self-respect. I am sorry, Louise. The harm was unintentional, but entirely my fault. Do you accept my apology?"

Two thoughts crowded into Louise's mind, the first was that Liam needed to shut up. Whatever he was blathering about, they could discuss later.

The second thought, more of a compulsion, was that her best work, her very best work, properly displayed before a segment of New York's most discerning appreciators of art, lay beyond the doors.

She didn't give a damn about the people, but her art—

"I want to see," she said, dragging Liam across the room. "I have to see them."

Liam went peacefully, a few people calling greetings.

When they reached the double doors, Louise was abruptly, unashamedly terrified. She buried her face against Liam's throat, his lacy jabot tickling her cheek.

"I thought they'd been d-destroyed," she whispered. "I asked for them back, from the galleries that had agreed to take them on commission, though it took me weeks to find the nerve. They all said the pieces were 'no longer in inventory.' I got a check, when what I wanted was my art back. I've always wanted my art back. I thought they'd all gone in d-dumpsters—"

"Look, Louise," Liam said softly, arms around her. "Every piece is whole and safe, and they're all here, except for one vase that I sent to a friend drowning in grief."

Louise couldn't hold on to Liam tightly enough, could not contain the singing, soaring joy, or the terror, of what he'd done.

"Show me, Liam."

An attendant opened the double doors, and Liam escorted her into a carpeted expanse of light and quiet. Her best work—vases, bowls, a whimsical teapot, a fan made of clay and northern lights, a dish wide enough to serve as a grinding stone, a matched set of tea cups…. Every piece accounted for, every piece perfectly lit to show off form and finish.

Louise knew which one Liam had sent to his friend: A vase about six inches tall that she'd named Consolation. In this room, Liam had assembled all of the rest. Her past, her future, her heart, all on display.

"They're beautiful," Louise said, wiping a tear away with the back of her wrist. "I was never sure. I thought maybe I'd not seen clearly, maybe memory played tricks, maybe merely pretty is all I'm capable of."

"You're capable of gorgeous, insightful, brilliant work, all of it," Liam said. "Not a runt in the litter, Louise Cameron, not a second best, not a single item that falls below the standard of the rest. You're not only a genius with color and shape, you're consistent. Larry O'Connor agreed when he was given a private showing this morning."

Louise leaned into Liam and wept, and she laughed, and she dreamed up all manner of new shapes and approaches to try. She was still giddy with sheer joy two hours later as the attendants began to discreetly murmur about the bar closing soon, and there being time for one last trip to the buffet.

"I don't want to leave this room, Liam," Louise said as she accepted a piece of tablet from him. "*I made this*, I made all of this, and it's good." She kissed him as sweetness suffused her. "You know what else, Cromarty? *I can make more.* I know that now. Purple is calling to me, like the heather. Purple and green have a lot to say to each other."

And Louise had more she'd say to Liam, when all these smiling, well-dressed people left them some privacy.

"Let's find a glass of champagne," Liam suggested, "because this was a successful show if ever I saw one."

"Larry O'Connor winked at me," Louise said, slipping out of her shoes as the textile artist waved good-bye. Louise was tipsy, though she'd not had even a glass of wine. "I want you to understand something, though, Liam Cromarty."

Liam collected her shoes. "Say my name like that in bed. You'll like the results."

He led her from the display room to the bar. Louise waited for their drinks while Liam found a place to stash her shoes.

"I feel like we should waltz on the roof or something," Louise said, passing Liam his champagne. She touched her glass to his. "To Scotland, the brave."

Liam kissed her, then took a sip, and set the drink aside. "I asked you earlier if you accepted my apology, Louise. May I take it you've responded in the affirmative?"

— ⟐ —

Louise had become like one of her vases, a pillar of grace and beauty, illuminated from within, imbued with motion even when she stood still.

"Let's find some ferns to hide behind," she said, taking Liam by the hand. "Understand this: You are being daft, and I love you for it, but enough is enough."

"I am daft," Liam said as they wound past the buffet and into a conversational grouping away from the brightest lights. Across the mezzanine, people were putting on wraps, security guards were looking relieved, and a wonderfully successful show was coming to an end.

The press had attended, and Liam would have a few more clients for this evening's work, about which, he cared not at all.

"I was mean to Robert," Louise said, stretching luxuriously.

"You were quite civil to him," Liam countered, lowering himself to the carpet beside her chair. "You asked about his latest publication then dodged off to say hello to the reigning queen of textile art."

Larry O'Connor had been trapped in a discussion of the symbolism of fur in colonial portraiture for another fifteen minutes while Liam had stayed at his lady's side.

"Naughty me," Louise said, admiring her own bare toes.

She could light up the Orkneys on New Year's Eve with that smile.

"Might I interrupt your naughtiness to trouble you for your opinion on another artist's work?" Liam asked.

Louise stroked his hair, the gentlest caress. "I'd give you pretty much anything you asked for, Liam Cromarty. I hadn't realized how I'd been grieving, not knowing what had happened to my art. Without the actual pieces, I had no evidence I'd ever created anything. Thank you from the bottom of my heart. The managing partner for the law firm that hosted this shindig asked if I accepted private commissions."

"You'll soon be wealthy if you said yes." And how pleased Liam would be, to see Louise's career restored to her in such abundance.

Louise dropped a kiss on his crown. "I am wealthy. I have good health, a ton of ideas, and good people in my life. The rest doesn't matter."

She didn't reiterate that she loved him. She'd lobbed that salvo at him when he'd been too drunk on the sight of her to respond, and then she'd nattered on about taking his clothes off.

Liam scooted around, so he was on his knees at her side. "You have something else, too, Louise."

"A sweet tooth. Or a tablet tooth."

"You have my heart," Liam said, extracting a ring box from a pocket. "You have my love. You have my loyalty, my fidelity, and most of my tablet stash for the rest of my natural days. My cat and my uncle have already switched their allegiance to you, and my dog is sure to follow."

Louise had gone still, her hand resting on his shoulder.

"Thank you, Liam. I love you, too. Very much."

"We thought we were done," he said. "You went off to law school, thinking you'd closed a chapter in your life forever. I settled into teaching and hoped I could be content. I don't want contentment, Louise, unless I can share it with you." He passed her the ring box. "What do you think of the setting?"

Louise opened the box and peered at the ring as if it might jump up and bite her nose. Liam kissed that nose instead.

"Will it do, Louise? Will I do?"

"Oh, Liam. Of course you'll do, but may I have the words, please?"

He assumed a proper kneeling posture. "Louise Cameron, will you marry me? Will you become my lawfully wedded wife, my best friend, my partner, lover, and companion in all things? I come with a lot of family and a stubborn streak."

She looped her arms around his shoulders. "Stubborn is good, Liam. Stubborn means we don't give up, we keep trying, we find a way to make our marriage work. I'll marry you, and you'll have a stubborn wife, too."

A yes, then. A beautiful, heartfelt, unhesitating yes. Louise had said yes to him, to his love, to a shared future. Liam stuffed the ring box in his pocket and slid the gold band around Louise's finger.

"I love it," she said, wiggling her fingers so the light caught the emerald.

"I love you." Liam had waited weeks to say that, the longest weeks of his life. "I love you, I love you. I love you, and I want an early wedding present."

"I gave you some early wedding presents this afternoon, Liam Cromarty."

*Had she ever.* Liam drew Louise to her feet. "And what lovely gestures those were. Now I want another kind of lovely gesture."

The recessed lighting around the mezzanine had dimmed, and staff were clearing off the buffet.

"Will I need my shoes?" Louise asked as Liam led her back to the display area.

"Not for this. I want a guided tour, Louise. I want to hear the story of each piece, to know what decisions you had to make, where the ideas came from, and what comes next."

"I know what comes next," she said, stopping before a loving cup with braided handles. The lights had been turned down in here too, and yet, the greens and golds of the glaze seemed to glow with warmth. "What comes next, Liam Cromarty, is we live happily ever after."

# EPILOGUE

—◦◦◦◦◦—

Every artist needed a spouse, a Liam Cromarty, to handle all the pesky financial details associated with sales, to offer the occasional—though never unsolicited—comment on a work in progress, and to impersonate a romantic bunny several times throughout the day.

Liam had the knack of leaving Louise alone her in studio precisely long enough to accomplish a goal, but not long enough for her to grow hungry or unproductive. He was often at work elsewhere in the house, grading papers, preparing for class, or transacting art rental business with clients a dozen time zones away.

Or, when the mood struck, cooking.

"You made sambusas," Louise said, snatching a clean towel from the stack near the work sink. "What do you want to bet Uncle Donald will be here in the next fifteen minutes?"

Liam set down a tray laden with a pile of golden, flakey sambusas, two bottles of Deuchars beer, and a roll of paper towels.

"Donald is off working on his golf game," Liam said. "Seems another one of your lawyer friends from Maryland has decided to come to Scotland for a golfing holiday."

Louise opened both bottles, taking a sniff of hop-py loveliness.

"The only lawyers in Maryland I'd call my friends are Dunstan and Jane." Mostly Jane, though Dunstan had grown on her. "I certainly know a few more, and most of them are decent people."

None of whom she missed.

Liam took a sip of his beer, and what did it say about a woman who'd been married for nearly two months, that she still found the sight of her husband *drinking beer* sexy?

Liam passed her two sambusas on a paper towel. "Shame on you. You know better than to look at me like that, Mrs. Cromarty."

*Mrs. Cromarty.* She was Louise Cameron Cromarty now, soon to be a master's degree candidate at the Glasgow School of Art. She and Liam had decided to first take a year to enjoy being married, and for Louise to settle into her Scottish home.

A fine plan, but like all plans…

"That's a lovely piece," Liam said, gesturing with his bottle at a pot Louise had taken from the kiln earlier in the day. "You meant what you said, about purple and green having a lot to say to each other, and the peach goes surprisingly well."

Louise took a bite of food still warm from the oven. "This is your best recipe yet. If you give it to Donald, he might leave us alone for more than three days at a time."

Though Louise knew why Donald was stopping by so often. Auld Donald was a canny fellow.

"A fine notion," Liam said, chewing contemplatively.

Marriage had changed him, added peacefulness to his quiet, and smiles to his conversation. Louise was about to upset that quiet, but also, she hoped, to inspire more smiles.

"Who's the next guest in the cottage?" she asked. "The bar association was full of golfers, though I had the sense they played mostly to get out of the office."

Niall Cromarty was the family golfer and Jeannie's brother.

He had Liam's broad shoulders, also a thriving little golf operation in the wilds of Perthshire, and form most pros could only envy.

Niall did not, however, lay claim to any charm.

"The next guest," Liam said, "is a lady by the name of Julie Leonard. She's quite focused on her golf apparently."

For a prosecutor, Julie had been pleasant to work with. "*Niall's* supposed to brave the midgies to take her golfing?"

"Which is why Jeannie sent Donald off to the links. One must always have a backup plan. I don't suppose you play?"

Plans again. *Please, Liam, be the kind of husband who can adjust to a change in plans.*

"I don't play golf worth a hoot," Louise said. "Niall might not make a bad golf buddy for Julie." Who was used to dealing with trial attorneys and criminals.

"He'll be awful," Liam said, finishing his first sambusa. "Niall's in want of cheer, unless you happen to be a drooling, cooing wee bairnie by the name of Henry."

Louise set her beer down after one sip. Deuchars had become her favorite, but she wouldn't be drinking much for the foreseeable future.

"Everybody can use a devoted uncle," Louise said, "or first cousin once removed."

Liam paused, his bottle halfway to his mouth, while Louise's heart turned over. She would recall this moment, just as she recalled the moment Liam had confused her for a little old lady at the airport. She had an entire mental portfolio of images of Liam, each one beloved. Arthur's Seat, Culloden, walking the banks of the river with Helen, their wedding day.

And their wedding night.

"Niall's first cousins once removed would be… *our children*," Liam said, peering at Louise.

"Got it in one, Mr. Cromarty. Don't suppose you've given any thought to names?"

Liam set his ale down carefully. "Louise?"

"That name's taken, and wouldn't work for a boy."

"Louise Cameron Cromarty. I've wondered what the change is. Your pots have gone from beautiful to sublime, and I didn't think holy matrimony the entire explanation."

The explanation sat across from her, smiling the sweetest, dearest, *hottest* smile.

"Expectant mothers nap a lot," Louise said. "I don't want to nap alone."

Liam grabbed the plate and both beers and nearly ran for the kitchen. Louise beat him to the bedroom, where they did, indeed, enjoy a nice long nap.

Eventually.

# AUTHOR'S NOTE

On one of my trips to Scotland, I crossed paths with fellow traveler Heitzi Epstein, a ceramic, jewelry and textile artist and teacher. Heitzi is also one of few people who really, truly knows what my foster care lawyer gig involves. In a past life she was the attorney in charge of the Child Welfare Project of the National Association of Child Advocates…. and she loves Scotland… and she loves music… and she lives in Maryland.

Yikes! No wonder the time spent with her inspired a story with a great big, pretty happily-ever-after ending. Heitzi was very helpful answering my questions about ceramics, though of course, any boo-boos are exclusively mine.

If you'd like to see some of Heitzi's creations, take a gander at her website at heitzi.com. I'm telling you, you meet the nicest people in Scotland…

If you enjoyed this wee dram of Scottish contemporary romance from Grace Burrowes, you might also enjoy the prequel novella, Kiss and Tell, or her Scottish Victorian series featuring the MacGregor brothers:

The Bridegroom Wore Plaid

Once Upon a Tartan

The MacGregor's Lady

What A Lady Needs for Christmas

Grace also has more contemporary romances out in 2015, including

A Single Kiss (January 2015)

The First Kiss (February 2015)

Kiss Me Hello (March 2015)

And she returns to Regency England with

The Duke's Disaster (April 2015)

Watch for the next novella in Grace's Highland Holidays series, Love on the Links, or sign up for her newsletter at www.graceburrowes.com/contact.php to be kept informed of new releases, exclusive content, giveaways, or the upcoming Scotland With Grace group tour.

# ABOUT GRACE BURROWES

**Grace Burrowes** loves to write, and has more than forty romance titles to her name. She's happiest when she's toddling around Scotland or Merry Olde, looking for story ideas and scarfing down whisky flavored tablet (sort of a sweetened condensed milk fudge/rocket fuel blend). Scottish traditional music, breathtaking rural scenery, and the odd friendly cat (waves at Tobermory) are among her dearest delights. When she's not wandering around the Highlands in the name of research for her books, she's a child welfare attorney practicing in Western Maryland. Grace loves to hear from her readers, and can be reached through her website at graceburrowes. com.

# The Laird and I

PATIENCE GRIFFIN

# DEDICATION

For Kate
Thank you, cousin, for being my traveling companion and
friend.
Let's always remember the Wallace and the Bruce and…
sheep!

Aye, it was grand!

# PRONUNCIATIONS:

**Braw**          brave, but also implies fine, splendid, or excellent

**Caber**          a roughly trimmed tree trunk used in the caber toss in the Scottish Highland games

**Céilidh**          (KAY-lee)—a party/dance

**Nansaidh**          (nan-say)

**nighean**          (nee-in) means daughter

**shite**          derogatory term

# CHAPTER ONE

"This can't be!" Sophie wiped the condensation away and pressed closer to the Land Rover's window.

She'd figured Hugh McGillivray's wool mill would be a shed and his house a lean-to. But at the gate entrance, she could see he had a castle! Kilheath Castle—if she was reading the sign correctly. On either side of the entrance stood two snow-dusted watchtowers with the wrought-iron gates hinged open. Quite a sight for a small town lass who was used to stone cottages and clapboard.

"Sophie? Are ye listening, lass?" her mama said from the front seat of the vehicle.

Her mama wasn't the only one in the car with her. Deydie, the village's matriarch and head quilter, had been lecturing Sophie, too, all the way from Gandiegow, her home on the northeast coast of Scotland.

"Aye, Mama, I'm listening."

Her mother, Annie, turned the car down the long lane leading up to Hugh's home. Conifers, tall and thick, hid the castle, which could be seen only at the bends in the road. Sophie cranked her head this way and that to make out the complete structure.

Apparently, neither her mother nor Deydie were impressed with the grounds or the view around them—they didn't gasp the way Sophie had—but the closer they maneuvered toward Hugh's house—correction, Hugh's castle—the more the lecture intensified.

"Make sure to do your bright-light therapy every day, nighean," Mama reminded her for the umpteenth time. "None of us want a relapse."

For God's sake, Sophie was twenty-five and able to care for herself. True, she'd suffered from SAD, seasonal affective disorder, her whole life. But now that she'd been diagnosed and treated, she felt so much better. Emma, Gandiegow's therapist, had agreed that Sophie was well enough to venture out and do something on her own…even though it was still January and the days were short. The winter months were no longer painful and full of despair for Sophie, now that she was using her bright-light lamp, which simulated sunshine. She felt fine. Wonderful actually. More like summer Sophie than the depressed mess she usually was this time of year.

"I'll be all right, Mama. I promise."

"But at any time, if you need me, just ring me up. I'll come straightaway and cart ye home," Annie said.

"Aye," Deydie chimed in. "Ye'll probably turn tail, but make sure ye have the woolens picked out first. We'll need those for the next quilting retreat."

Deydie made it sound like Sophie wouldn't last the night, but she held her tongue. Deydie was a force to be reckoned with, especially if she had her broom nearby to take a swing at you.

"Ye don't have to do this," Annie said. From this angle Sophie could tell her mama was chewing her lower lip again.

"But I do." Sophie had promised. She'd told Hugh McGillivray by email that she'd housesit for him. She'd also promised Deydie that she'd apprentice with the kiltmaker at Hugh's woolen factory for the next week. "It's all set. The plans are made."

"But…if—" her mother started again.

"Dammit, Annie, stop hovering," Deydie barked. She had a way of knocking you off guard and keeping ye on edge. "The lass needs to put her talents to good use. She's a hell of a stitcher. Ye know why we need her to expand her skills. When I almost didn't get Dominic's kilt in time for Christmas, I made a decision. And when I make a decision, by goodness, it's going to get done—Sophie here, will become Gandiegow's new kiltmaker." The old woman wrenched her head around to bark at Sophie, too. "Kiltmaking would be one hell of a skill to bring to the table. Maybe run retreats where you can teach the craft to others."

"We'll see." Sophie concentrated on the view instead of the lecture.

"There's no we'll see about it, girl." Deydie faced forward and nodded her head with finality. "Ye'll do it."

Sure, Sophie wanted to learn the art of kiltmaking—she was just sick to death of being told what to do.

A second structure came into view, opposite the castle, high on a hill—a ruin. A fence had been placed around the stone fortress, but some of the walls still stood proudly, stretching to the sky. First chance she had, winter or not, Sophie would explore every inch of it. The stones had withstood centuries of dark seasons and needed no bright lights to shore them up.

Deydie harrumphed, her signature sound, a cross between an angry walrus and a beached whale. "Aye, ye'll apprentice with the kiltmaker while ye're housesitting. But just as importantly, we're all counting on ye to use that good eye of yours to find us some nice wool oddments. The wool quilt retreat is in six weeks, and we'll need every remnant you can lay your hands on."

"Fine. I'll pick out some top-quality remnants."

Gandiegow had been building up its reputation as the quilting destination in the Highlands. Everyone in the village contributed. Up until now, Sophie had been unable to do much, especially in the winter months, but now that she was better, she was eager to do her part and give back to the community.

She didn't say any more to her mother and Deydie, only stared out the window as Hugh's castle grew and the snow-covered gardens came into view.

She'd met Hugh last summer when he came to Gandiegow's midsummer céilidh and dance. Amy, Sophie's good friend and Hugh's cousin, had insisted that she and Hugh were perfect for each other and that dancing at the céilidh would be the ideal time to bring them together. Amy and Hugh may have been raised together by their aunt—as close as any brother and sister—but apparently, Amy didn't know squat about Hugh now that he was grown. He wasn't the fun-loving, happy-go-lucky lad that Amy described. He'd been an irritatingly handsome brute, who couldn't be bothered to dance with Sophie, even though Amy had insisted.

Sophie had shown him. It had been July, when the days were long with her seasonal depression in remission. She'd exacted revenge by flirting with every eligible man in the room, danced with as many of the fishermen that she could coax out onto the floor, and had finally persuaded Ramsay Armstrong to walk her home...making sure that Hugh saw that she'd left with another man. But Sophie and Ramsay were only friends. Hugh also didn't know that Ramsay didn't date the lasses from Gandiegow—too much gossip for him. Besides, Sophie had never seen Hugh again. Although, she'd thought many times about his handsome face and that look of confusion and pain that had been painted there as she'd sashayed out the door.

Sophie twisted the Munro tartan scarf in her lap. *Thank goodness, I won't have to see him now.*

Actually, she'd been shocked when Amy had mentioned this housesitting gig. She'd been even more shocked when she'd received an email from Hugh himself. He'd been surprisingly pleasant over the Internet, explaining that he'd be in America for the next week, and would she mind watching his house for him? Perfect timing, as far as Sophie was concerned. She was more than ready for an adventure, to do something on her own. A lass of twenty-five needed breathing room from her parents. And her village!

Annie pulled the car to the front of Hugh's home and turned off the engine. She let out a low whistle. "'Tis beautiful."

"It's too big for any one person," Deydie said. "A lass could lose herself in a place like this."

Sophie was counting on it. She was here on a mission to reinvent herself—ready to prove to everyone that she was capable...now that she was doing better.

She pulled out the email with the instructions on it, though she knew every word by heart. "The key is under the small bird statue on the porch."

As she got out, the cold January breeze blew her in the direction of the castle and the many steps that led up to the massive oak double doors. Beside the entry was a stone table, and on top of the table was a small stone bird. But she didn't immediately run up the salted stairs and retrieve the key. Instead, she permitted herself a quick spin to take in the panoramic of the castle, the gardens, the loch, and the hills, before trekking to the back of the vehicle to unload her luggage.

Annie stood beside the SUV, chewing her lip. Deydie, though, gazed up at the castle. Was the old woman itching to get inside and take a look around? But Sophie wanted this place to herself. Queen of the castle, as it were.

She shivered a little, standing at the bottom of the steps with her luggage around her. "Well, ye better hurry to Inverness, you two, if ye're going to get those supplies before the shops close." And before they all froze to death! Sophie made sure that her voice sounded as chipper and firm as the columns she stood by. "Here, Mama, let me give you a hug goodbye."

Annie's face twisted in conflict.

Separation anxiety. Emma had warned Sophie about it, but encouraged her to not be deterred.

Sophie wrapped her mother in her arms, feeling it, too. That pull to still be the little girl, and at the same time, a woman on her own. "I'll be fine, Mama. I promise."

Deydie tugged on her mother's arm. "We best be getting on the road. We'll have the devil of a time making it, especially if there are cattle in the road. Hairy beasts."

Annie let go, but the tears swimming in her eyes had Sophie close to inviting them in for a cuppa. Then the strangest thing happened. Deydie reached out and touched Sophie's cheek, something the tough Scottish woman had never done before. But if Sophie had expected soft and kind words to come from the matriarch's mouth, she was mistaken.

"Pick out some damned good woolens, or else ye'll be meeting with the business end of me broom when ye get home."

Sophie secured her tartan scarf more firmly around her neck. Deydie's hard words had only made it easier to see them go. As the Land Rover made its way down the driveway, Sophie didn't budge. As soon as the car was out of sight, she ran up the front steps and pulled out the key from under the stone bird.

The email had listed a few chores that were to be done daily, but to a woman who hailed from Gandiegow, the list looked comparatively like a vacation. The first thing was to introduce herself to Hugh's dogs, Scottish deerhounds, who were penned up in the back. However, when she unlocked the door, she was met by the two gentle giants.

"Hey, boys," she said. Hugh had told her they weren't aggressive, which was a blessing since they were almost three feet tall and close to her in weight.

"What are ye doing inside if the master isn't home?"

A sinking feeling came over her. What if she'd gotten the days mixed up? What if Hugh was here? She glanced at the empty driveway. Her mother was gone, and she had no way of getting home. She checked the dates on the email.

"It all looks good." She scratched one of the boys behind the ears. "So which one of you is the Wallace and which one of you is the Bruce?" As she read the tags on their collars, she gave them each a hug. "I guess the master decided to leave you inside to wait for me. Come on. Help me get settled."

The dogs followed her as she carried her things into the castle, but she stopped abruptly at the ornately carved woodwork in the entryway. She took it all in—the dark crown molding, the wainscoting, the bannisters of the dual staircase. She reached out to touch the stag carved into the baluster, feeling the wood comfort her as much as any natural light. Expensive-looking vases lined tables down the hallway, and massive painted portraits hung on the walls. The castle was part museum and part home. It was ostentatious, and Sophie loved it.

Hugh had left instructions for her to stay in his room. When she'd responded that she couldn't possibly, he'd insisted. *The view from my room mustn't be missed.*

She dragged her luggage upstairs to the third floor and found his room, dropping her things in the doorway.

"Ohmigod."

The four-poster bed was anchored with what looked like cabers and positioned at an angle so the occupant of the bed could enjoy the magnificent view. Diagonally across the room from the bed were two picture windows that hugged the corner. If both of the windows were undraped. She pulled back the curtain to see the sunlight glinting off the snow and ice-covered loch, peaceful and tranquil. The other window framed a Munro, a true Scottish mountain, with its peaks white and tall.

Sophie felt a special connection to all the Munros in Scotland as she was a direct descendent of Sir Hugh Munro who had climbed and categorized most of the elevations.

She could almost imagine what the Munro would look like in the spring—lush green and scattered with white, black-faced sheep grazing at the lower levels.

"Oh, that would be a sight to see," she said to the Wallace.

She stepped back and collapsed on the bed. The Wallace and the Bruce jumped up, joining her, making themselves comfortable on the king-sized pillows propped at the head.

"I could get used to living like this!" She centered herself between the dogs, enjoying the incredible view outside. "I'm going to love it here." The Bruce inched closer so he could get his belly rubbed, too. For a few moments, she allowed herself to relax, but only for a few.

"Come on, fellas. Things have to get done. Let's find yere water dishes, and then I'll make myself familiar with the rest of the house."

The dogs followed her back downstairs. Sophie had the place to herself. According to the email, the house staff left early on Saturdays and was off tomorrow, too. This would be her only chance to explore the house without an audience. Come Monday morning, Sophie was expected at the kiltmaker's to begin her apprenticeship, and to meet the other workers at the wool mill.

She spent the rest of the day in glorious, quiet contentment, without another soul to tell her what to do. Cabbage and tattie soup had been left for her in the refrigerator of the professional-looking kitchen, along with a covered loaf of thick-crusted bread and a knife to cut it with. She fixed a tray and took it into the parlor, turning on all the lights. The winter days were short in the Highlands, the sun fully down by four. She cuddled with the dogs in front of a roaring fire while she ate her dinner.

Very unexpectedly, she felt lonely

"I've never been away from home before," she said to the dogs beside her.

Black clouds—very familiar and unwelcome—started to

cover her. Emma had drilled into her time and time again to be proactive with her depression. As soon as the first wave of despair hit, Sophie was to plug in her therapy lamp.

The dogs followed her to the small writing table as she set up her bright-light lamp. She grabbed a tweed fashion magazine off the shelf behind her and sat browsing through it while soaking up the light.

As both dogs lay on the floor beside her, she rubbed them with her socked feet. "Ye two have to keep me from calling home to Mama. She would be nothing but worried and full of instructions for me." The Wallace stood and rested his head in Sophie's lap.

"Ye're both good boys."

After a long while, she felt better and made her way upstairs with the Wallace and the Bruce following. They watched as she unpacked her things into the three drawers that Hugh had cleared for her. Within a half hour, she had her nightgown on, her teeth brushed, and was tucked under the quilts with the dogs beside her.

Being in an unfamiliar bed should've felt strange. Somehow, though, she was comforted. It was either the dogs keeping her company or Hugh's aftershave, which lingered in the room. She was on her own…for the first time in her life.

She reached over, flipped off the side lamp, and settled further under the quilts. The Wallace scooted closer, cuddling into her back. The Bruce stretched across the bottom of the bed by her feet.

But the darkness and the quiet brought back the conversation she'd overheard last night between her parents.

"It's too late for her. She's past her prime," Sophie's father said, much to her dismay. Her da was a good da. Why would he say such a thing?

"It's never too late, if the right one comes along," Annie argued.

"But she's too old. Too bossy. Too set in her ways. No one

will want her now." Her da had sighed heavily. "I know ye like to believe in romantic ideas, luv, but ye need to face facts."

Annie had agreed, and Sophie had been heartbroken.

But now she was accepting her future. She didn't need love to make her happy. She reached back and gave the Wallace a squeeze.

Because the day had been long and the dogs were so warm and reassuring, Sophie fell fast asleep.

She woke in the middle of the night, her heart pounding. Had the bed dipped down? There had certainly been some movement. But then she remembered the dogs. She smiled into the darkness, feeling foolish—one of them must've readjusted. But then she heard a deep sigh. A deep, male sigh. That is definitely no dog.

"Move over, Wallace," the voice said.

Oh, God, the master is home!

Sophie froze. But her nerves were in a jumble—terrified.

What is Hugh doing home?

Why would he come and get in bed with me after insisting that I sleep here?

A million other questions bombarded her. His aftershave floated her way and hovered, adding to her confusion.

"Walllllace," he said again firmly. She could feel the dog being pushed over. "If ye don't make room for me, ye'll be sleeping with the rams in the sheep shed."

This time, both dogs rose, circled in a C, and the other plopped down over her legs, trapping her.

Oh, crud! Without the dog barrier, Hugh could stretch out and touch her.

Could she get her feet loose without anyone noticing— man or beast?

For a long time, she didn't move. She lay barely breathing, trying to decipher the different noises in the night. The dogs were both snoring. She was sure the master had gone to sleep, too. She took her chance.

By millimeters, she pulled her feet free and began to scoot to the edge of the mattress. So slowly in fact, it might turn morning before she made it out. She kept her senses tuned to the opposite side of the bed. Just as she was about to lower her feet to the floor and slip away, a strong hand reached over and gripped her thigh.

"Who are you?" he growled, more feral than any dog in the vicinity. "And why in the deuce are you in my bed?"

She bit her lip to keep from squeaking, but then finally spoke. "It's me, Sophie."

"Sophie?" He sounded completely clueless. "Sophie, who?"

"Sophie Munro."

As she heard him groping for the lamp on his side of the bed, the hand gripping her thigh held on tighter. The light came on.

"Amy's friend?" she added, like she wasn't sure Amy was really her friend or not.

He glared at her as if the Loch Ness Monster had crawled into his bed.

And that's when the quilt slipped on his side of the bed. The brute was naked.

# CHAPTER TWO

"How did you get in here?" Hugh held on to the woman beside him. It registered that her skin was soft and warm, but he could see only bluidy red. "What do ye want?" He slightly shook her leg.

She pushed at his arm. "Let go of me!"

It was one thing for him to be holding on to her. It was quite another to have her touching him back. He let go and swung his legs over the side of the bed, sitting up and making sure the quilt kept him covered.

She averted her eyes anyway.

"Tell me why ye're in my bed." He noticed his hounds had ratcheted themselves up against her as if protecting her from him! Gads! "Wallace. Bruce. Come." He pointed to the floor beside him.

The Wallace whimpered, and she wrapped her arms around them. "Stop being a bully."

"Good God." He glared at her and then at his animals. "Biscuit?"

Both dogs' ears popped up. They jumped off the bed and ran to him, sitting by his feet at attention.

"Close yere mouth, lassie. In fact, close yere eyes while

ye're at it. I'm not decent here, and I'd like to be."

When she turned away from him, he grabbed his boxers off the chair and slipped them on. His dogs were still waiting, so he pulled two biscuits from his jeans pocket. "Here, ye disloyal bastards." For a moment, his eyes searched her backside, trying to outline the body that lay beneath her cotton nightgown. Aye, he remembered Sophie. She was as appealing now as she had been back in the summer. He felt the same instant attraction. Maybe stronger. But he couldn't think about her that way now.

The reflection in the picture windows shifted, catching his attention. Sophie was staring back at him, her mouth shaped into an O. She'd been watching his every move. She seemed particularly interested in his lower half.

"Did ye get an eyeful, lass?"

Her eyes shot up to his. Her teeth caught her bottom lip. For a second, they stared at each other, before she averted her gaze. She squared her shoulders and faced him, that exposed look gone.

"I've seen hundreds of naked men."

He grabbed his jeans off the chair and slipped them on. "Hundreds?"

"Aye." She waved her hand like she was airbrushing him. "Nothing new there." But her cheeks were bright red, and he'd bet his best weaving machine that he'd been her first.

With her facing him, he could now take in the terrain under her shift a bit easier. She was perfectly proportioned, but maybe not as breasty as he'd like. Her nipples budding against the fabric of her nightgown did intrigue him more than he wanted them to.

"Put a robe on," he growled.

She clutched the quilt up to her chin. "I didn't bring one. I was supposed to be here alone."

He snatched up his discarded flannel shirt and tossed it to her. "Here."

She caught it. "Turn around first."

"You just ogled my naked arse, and ye're ordering me to turn around over a couple of perky nipples?"

She clutched his shirt to her chest, blushing red all the way to her cheeks.

And because he could be a son of a bitch sometimes, he went ahead and scandalized her further. "I'm not lying when I tell you I've seen plenty of naked women, hundreds even." If magazines counted.

Goldilocks glared at him, a bit of a stare-down, but he held his ground. In the end, he won, too. She gave him her back while she slipped his shirt over her nightgown.

His shirt swam on her, and the strangest thing happened— something quite uncomfortable shifted in his chest. He had the awful urge to beg her to come closer, stand before him... but not like one of his dogs. He merely wanted her near enough that he could touch her.

His oversized bedroom was abruptly much too small and cozy. "Follow me," he said.

She cleared her throat with a little, "Ahem."

"Could you put a robe on?" she said shyly.

She was sweet, and her embarrassment was damned attractive. He shook his head exaggeratedly, as if he were a man whose patience had been tested.

"A little man chest bothers ye, after a hundred naked men?"

She donned her gumption like it was his shirt. "I've seen more than enough men, thank you very much."

Aye, me. He opened his armoire and pulled out a T-shirt and slipped it on. "Better?"

"Much," she said. "Come, Wallace. Come, Bruce. The master has something to say."

His damned hounds lumbered after her bare feet. Those two disloyal bastards needed a long visit at obedience school, at least when it comes to remembering who gives the orders around here. "The upper solarium is to yere right."

For a moment, he stood in his room alone and felt that everything had changed.

He padded into the solarium after her, as bad as his dogs, and found the Wallace and the Bruce beside her with her feet curled under her on the sofa. Making herself at home.

She stifled a long yawn.

He stayed standing, hoping to reestablish that he was indeed the master of his castle. "Now, tell me why ye're in my house." And why you were in my bed.

She screwed up her face, and the place between her eyebrows pinched together. "Because you hired me to be here?" Her voice held a heaping dollop of attitude.

"I what?" he said incredulously.

She popped up. "Wait here." The dogs went to follow, but she put her hand out in the stay position. A moment later, she was back. She thrust a piece of paper at him. "There. In your own words."

He looked at the email. "What is this?" He scanned all the way down. "I—I…"

"Amnesia?" she provided. She looked quite pleased with herself, perched again on his couch, taking the stance of a vindicated woman. Vixen.

He bore into her with his eyes, quite deliberately, so she would shrink under his gaze. She didn't. He pointed the paper at her. "I've never seen this before in my life."

That did the trick. She withered a bit and uncurled her feet, setting them on the floor. "But—but that means that I'm…"

"Trespassing?" he finished, giving her the smuggest look he could conjure. "Aye."

---

Friggin', frackin', fuck. Sophie's mama wouldn't approve of her swearing, not even in her thoughts, but—damn! Emma, her therapist, had prepared her for a lot of different scenarios, but being caught in Hugh's bed—with her half-dressed and him completely naked—hadn't been one of them. Neither

her mama nor Emma had told her how to handle seeing a gorgeous man's full-monty reflection in the picture windows either. Oh, my! Sophie fanned herself, though there was a chill in the room.

Delayed, she jumped to her feet, more embarrassed than she'd been in her whole life. "Sorry." She'd have to pass Hugh to make a run for it, but there was no helping it. She didn't make eye contact, but put her head down and started for the door.

"Sophia."

His deep burr curled and hugged her given name soundly, too intimate for late night, too much for her senses. It made her pause as each syllable registered low in her middle. As she tried to slip past, Hugh grabbed her arm gently.

"Ye needn't tear out in the middle of the night, lass."

His breath hit her cheek. Her arm tingled where he held her. She wanted to go up on tippy-toes and find out what it would be like to kiss him.

He must've read her mind, for he dropped his hand and stepped away.

Great! Rejected once again by the insufferably gorgeous Hugh McGillivray.

"Come." He stepped from the solarium.

For a second, she wondered if he had been speaking only to the dogs, for they trotted after him.

He stuck his head back in. "I mean you, lass."

She followed and found him retrieving an old-fashioned skeleton key from a little basket that hung by the room next to his. For a second, he gazed upon the key and then determinedly shoved it into the opening and turned the lock. He pushed the door wide, flipped on the light, and stood back for her to enter.

The room was large like Hugh's, but not decorated in masculine tones. This room was all pink and floral—rose wallpaper, a gingham bedspread, rose motif pillows, and a matching sage afghan across the bottom of the bed. The Wallace and the Bruce slipped past Sophie and circled the room reverently.

"Whose room is this?"

Her eyes fell to the key grasped in his hand. The key shook with a slight tremor.

"It was my sister's." He frowned like he wanted to back out of the room and pretend he'd never unlocked the door.

Sophie knew all about his sister—falling through the ice on the loch, the drowning—the reason he'd gone to live with Amy and their aunt when he was twelve. His parents had been so distraught that Aunt Davinia had rescued him from his family's grief. Amy had said Hugh took a long time to recover, but he finally learned to laugh again, the two cousins having grand times together.

"Isn't there another room?" Sophie couldn't stay in this room. "Anything will do."

"Nay. After my parents…" he trailed off, but then changed tracks. "All the rooms have been cleared for redecorating. There's not another bed in the house. None, except mine and Chrissa's." His voice caught on his sister's name.

She touched his arm.

He jerked away as if her hand could scorch. "Stay. The room's just going to waste."

Chrissa's bedroom looked regularly maintained, not a speck of dust anywhere.

Sophie couldn't go back to his warm bed, and she certainly didn't want to sleep in a room that caused him pain.

"Good night," he said abruptly, leaving the key on the dresser. He was gone.

The Wallace and the Bruce looked conflicted.

"Go on now. Go sleep with the master."

They each gave her one more worried glance and then trotted from the room.

For a long moment, Sophie stood in the middle of the

floral paradise—perfectly feminine, perfectly preserved. When the quiet had thoroughly settled over her, she pulled the sage afghan from the bed, left the key on the dresser, and stepped into the hallway. She walked over to Hugh's closed door and laid a hand on it, worrying about the grief that she'd dredged up in him. But she didn't knock, knowing he didn't want comfort.

She sneaked down to the parlor to the loveseat in front of the fireplace. She wished now the dogs had stayed with her for company. When she lay down, the puzzle still remained—Amy had suggested that she housesit, but who had written those emails?

And more important, what would she do now?

—◦◦◦◦◦—

Morning came too soon. Hugh rolled over and swore, because last night he hadn't slept well. All he wanted to do this morning was to have a lie-in. But it was Sunday. And light was pouring into his room. "What the…?"

He sat up. The window overlooking the loch is uncovered? It was never uncovered! Why had Sophie pulled back the drape? The view was more than he could handle. Especially in the dead of winter!

He stomped to the window and yanked the curtain closed. While he was there, he pulled the drape on the Munro as well.

He fell back into bed, but he still had the same problem as he'd had last night. His bed smelled like the woman who slept in the room next to his, and he still didn't know how she'd ended up here.

The Wallace began to whine, and like clockwork, the Bruce started in, too.

"Good God!" The woman and beasts were out to get him. "Can't a man get any rest in his own house?" Maybe he'd let the dogs out and leave them in the cold for a good long while. That would teach them to drag him out of bed early. Even better, maybe he should put them in with Sophie and she could deal with their morning routine.

Hugh rolled out of bed again, went to his dresser, and pulled open the top drawer. He stared in disbelief. Lady things stared back—lacy, sexy bits of intrigue and color. With one index finger, he scooped up a turquoise thong that was erotic to look at, and soft to the touch, and didn't exactly match who he thought Sophie Munro was. He dropped it back into the mix and slammed the drawer shut. He opened the second drawer only to find bras and wool socks. The bras ranged from black to brightly colored, and he slammed that drawer as well.

The Bruce whined loudly this time.

"I'm trying, dammit. I can't verra well take ye out with naked feet." Hugh pulled open the third drawer and found women's jeans on one side and sweaters on the other. "What the hell is going on here? Sophie has certainly made herself at home." Had she decided to move in forever? In the closet, two dresses were hanging, while his shirts had been pushed to one side. He found his socks, skivvies, and other folded clothes thrown into a basket and deposited at the back of the closet. "Good God. Is nothing sacred?" He dug out a pair of socks for himself and quickly dressed. All the while, he groused loud enough to their adjoining wall to make sure his houseguest woke up.

Out in the hall, he was surprised she hadn't come out to see what the ruckus was all about. Why was the lass still abed? Had she had trouble sleeping, too? He decided to leave her be and deliberately passed her doorway without another glance. Downstairs, the leashes weren't hanging by the back door where he'd left them yesterday. He searched the kitchen first and then went to the parlor to see if Sophie had left them there.

Hugh didn't find the leashes, but found Goldilocks on the loveseat fast asleep. He would've liked to have had a few seconds to gaze upon her longer, but the Bruce and the Wallace wanted her attention. Each of them nudged her and licked her face.

"Off with ye," she laughed, coming awake. She sobered quickly when she saw Hugh, tugging the green afghan around her.

"I'm glad ye're awake, Sleeping Beauty. Yere loyal servants would like to relieve themselves, but their leashes have gone missing."

Sophie made an O with her delectable lips and reached around her, shoving her hand into the sofa cushions. "They're right here."

Hugh adjusted the pillows in the wing chair. In this house things were always put back in their place. What he'd seen of Sophie so far screamed disorder. Her tussled hair, her skewed nightdress, and the chaotic emotions she brewed up in him.

He took the leashes from her. "The room abovestairs wasn't to yere liking?" He should've been more polite—say good morning first, before starting the interrogation—but the woman had disrupted his sleep.

The hounds jumped up on either side of her, acting as if they were Yorkie pups, trying to crawl into her lap. She hugged them to her.

"Down, you two," he said.

The dogs didn't budge.

Hugh gave the command again, pointing to the floor this time, and they both hopped off and sat in front of him, obediently. Now, if he could only get the woman to obey him, too.

"I suggest while I walk the lads that you toddle upstairs and ready yereself for church."

"Church?"

"Aye. The place with the pews and the preacher." He snapped a leash on each dog. "I don't know what ye heathens do along the northeast coast, but us God-fearing Scots in the Grampians go to church on Sundays."

"Pretty cheeky for this early in the morn, Hugh," she

countered, rising.

"On our way to the kirk, we're going to discuss how you came to be in my bed."

She momentarily anchored her hands on her hips...until she apparently realized her nightgown wasn't nearly covering her perfect little breasts and that Hugh was an opportunistic bastard, feasting his eyes on her.

She snatched up his flannel shirt from the loveseat and huffed from the room. "Ye would think that a man who owned a castle would be more of a gentleman."

"Hurry up now," he called after her. "Dress warmly. We'll leave in the next thirty minutes." He laughed openly as her grumbles continued up two flights of stairs.

The Wallace had wiggled his way under Hugh's hand, and Hugh hadn't even realized the mutt was there. The dog looked up at him with consternation.

"I know, lad. I shouldn't be throwing petrol on the fire." The Bruce head-butted his other hand, wanting attention, too. "But I can't help myself. There's something about that lass when she's throwing flames."

Sophie didn't take the full thirty minutes to dress. After Hugh's brisk walk with the dogs down the lane and back, he found Sophie in the kitchen making tea. She was wearing a vintage wool dress with a million buttons up the front. On her feet she had an old-fashioned pair of lace-up boots. She was a woman out of time and en vogue—classic, a woman from the past, but one who could walk the runway of a London wool-revival fashion show. Hell, he could hire her to be one of the lasses to model his woolens. Her long blond hair cascaded down one shoulder, making Hugh want to run his hands through the golden strands. He had many impure thoughts—that he shouldn't have, especially right before church—so he stepped into the kitchen, making himself known.

"Did ye make enough for two, since you've made yereself at home?"

She went right on rattling the porcelain and rifling his drawers, the epitome of cheek and sass.

"Aye." Finally, she shrugged. "I thought ye might be cold after walking the dogs. Sit yereself down, and I'll pour."

Hugh opened the bread box and pulled out the oatcakes that Mrs. McNabb had left for him. Because things were becoming a little too domesticated and because he needed to remind Sophie that this was his house—his domain—he started up the interrogation once again. "Tell me, Sophie Munro, how is that ye've come to take up residence here?"

She ran her thumb over the edge of the silver butter knife. "Amy."

"Amy?" He was getting a small idea of what was going on.

"Aye. She told me ye were needing a house sitter for the next week. She said that ye wanted me to do it."

Sophie set his steaming mug in front of him.

"And ye believed her? I barely know you." Which wasn't really true. He knew a lot about Sophie Munro. Amy had tried to set them up last summer, and she'd told Hugh everything there was to know about the lively lass in front of him now. But Hugh hadn't been in any shape to court anyone. Especially one so lovely as she was.

"Nay. I didn't believe her. But I received several emails from you. I showed you only one last night. I have the rest in my bag. Upstairs." She set the sugar and milk at his elbow, but didn't pour herself a cup. "I'll get my things from yere room when we get back from church."

Damned straight, ye will! It was his house.

She gathered the dog dishes and filled them with water—as if it were her house, too.

He ignored the good care she gave his hounds. "Aye. I'd like to read those emails that I wrote."

"Oh, ye were kind and charming. Very helpful, ye were. Ye told me where to find the key. Told me to help myself to yere food. Even told me I was to take yere bed. For the view."

"Helpful, kind, and charming," he repeated. "That Amy needs to be turned over my knee for a good spanking."

Sophie sat the bowls before the dogs and slung a dishtowel over her shoulder exactly like his mum used to do. "Don't be angry with Amy. She's a mama now. A good one."

"She certainly thought she had the right to meddle." Both Amy and his aunt.

Sophie glanced at her watch. "You said we had thirty minutes before church. We best be going."

"Aye."

She twisted her watch. "I'll call my mother afterwards to come get me." She looked like more was bugging her than being sent on a fool's errand. She seemed to be conflicted about going home.

"What's wrong, lass?"

"Ye wouldn't understand."

—⁓⌘⁓—

No. A man like Hugh McGillivray wouldn't understand what it was like for Sophie to finally be on her own. Her freedom had lasted less than twenty-four hours. Deydie's veiled prediction that she would turn tail had come true. Sophie couldn't tell the man beside her either. Hugh had been to the far reaches of the world. And Sophie…well, she'd been nowhere.

She grabbed her coat from the hook at the back door, where she'd stowed it yesterday—when she'd pretended this was her house…her castle for the next week. Now, today, she was going home.

She laid her hand on the doorknob and looked back as Hugh downed the rest of his tea. He unfolded himself from the chair and followed her out.

The drive was empty. "Where's yere car? The barn?"

"We'll walk," he said. "It's a mile or so. The weather is only a wee bit chilly."

She marched out, glad she'd put on warm tights with her

dress. Hugh walked in silence beside her. Sophie waited for him to question her more about why she was there, but she had to know one thing before returning home.

"This may be too personal, but since we've already been in bed together, and I've added to the sights I've seen," she braved, referring to his naked backside, "why didn't you turn the light on when you came to bed last night? It might've clued me in sooner that you were there and vice versa."

He gazed off in the distance as if the answer lay beyond the Munro. "It's my habit." He seemed closed on the subject. But a moment later, he was asking a question of her. "Is there some reason why you don't want to go home?"

Sophie couldn't tell him the complete truth, but she could share a sliver of it. "Ye've made arrangements for me to apprentice with yere head kiltmaker for the next week. Or whoever sent those emails did." Then the reality hit. "Or maybe the phantom emailer was pulling the sheep's wool over my eyes on that, too."

"We'll find out soon enough. Willoughby will be at the kirk. He's been at McGillivray's House of Woolens since the day he was born, and he's at least eighty years old, if he's a day."

One thing would be cleared up soon.

"Why else don't you want to go home?"

She kicked a loose rock. She wasn't willing to confess how being here was an adventure for her. He would laugh at her inexperience. But she could tell him about the task she'd been given. "You remember Deydie from when ye came to Gandiegow? The old woman who runs everything?"

"Aye. The crotchety ol' bat."

"She's not that bad. Deydie comes off as crusty as a barnacle and as tough as an old sailor, but she has a good heart."

"I only remember she gave me an earful about Amy. That I should do better about staying in touch. That family was more important than any business I had to run."

"Sounds like Deydie." Sophie envied the geese flying overhead. They were free to see the world with no one telling them what to do. "Well, Deydie's the one who wants me to take up kiltmaking. I can't stress to ye enough how much I don't want to disappoint her."

Hugh glanced over, as if to see if she was telling the truth. "And the rest of it?"

Not all of it, but some. "Deydie is also counting on me to come home with some woolen remnants, whatever quality wool piece you can spare. Gandiegow's Kilts and Quilts is running its first-ever wool quilt retreat in six weeks."

"We have plenty of oddments that should work." Hugh took her arm and guided her around a frozen puddle.

His grip was comforting, and she had the urge to lean into him. For a moment, she forgot what they were talking about.

"I can pick you out some nice pieces before you go." His words snapped her back to the conversation.

"Oh, no. I'm supposed to do the picking!" She had to be the one to do it. With kiltmaking off the table, the haul of remnants was the only way to contribute to Gandiegow now. And by God, she would do it.

At the Y in the road, Hugh changed the subject.

"There." He pointed down the lane to a group of five or so quaint stone buildings. One of them had a waterwheel. A little bridge was positioned over a stream with two cottages on the other side. "That's the wool mill. Of course, those two cottages over there belong to Willoughby and Magnus."

Hugh turned in the opposite direction. "The kirk is this way."

Sure enough, the church was down the road, with a small town beyond. The church was made of whitewashed stone and had a gray slate roof. Around the perimeter was a fenced-in cemetery with ancient headstones. The building looked older than the Munro behind it.

Hugh glanced down at her, and once again, Sophie was

caught off guard at how masculine and beautiful the man could be. She shivered.

"Ye're freezing," he said, mistaking her reaction to him for chilliness. He put his hand on her back and hurried her along. "I should've brought the car."

"I'm fine," she argued, but only halfheartedly. She felt right toasty with his hand firmly on her back. Luckily for her, he kept it there the rest of the way.

As they entered the building, the locals turned to stare—an elderly couple with matching Buchanan plaid scarves, a young mother with a babe propped on her hip, and two matronly women. All were gape-mouthed. Hugh dropped his hand and nodded to each one, almost as if he was daring them to ask what he was doing with the female beside him.

"There's Willoughby and Magnus," he said. "The wool brothers."

Sophie didn't get a chance to ask him what he meant as he ushered her to them. The two men stood four feet apart and were indeed prehistoric. They both had bushy white hair, slight paunches at their middles, and frowns on their faces.

Hugh leaned down and spoke conspiratorially to her. "They're feuding again. I'll introduce ye to Willoughby first. Magnus will have to wait."

As they approached, the taller of the two pointed at Sophie. "Is this her then, Laird?"

"Aye. Sophie, this is Willoughby, our master kiltmaker." Hugh studied the old man's face. "Then ye do know that she's come to apprentice with you?"

Willoughby looked as if the younger man had grown a horn from the middle of his head. "Of course, I do. Ye make me use that blasted computer, and I read yere blasted email on the matter." He huffed as if a shovel had been placed in his hands and he'd been forced to do hard labor. "She's to be here for the next week. Ye told me to clear my schedule to teach her everything I know." The old man shook his head and grumbled, "It'd take more than a week, a lifetime perhaps."

Hugh turned to Sophie and began unwinding her scarf from around her neck. "Ye're staying. Don't call home."

Before she could process his words—she was pretty damned distracted by him removing her scarf—old man Willoughby jabbed a finger in her face.

"Tomorrow morning, be on time," the kiltmaker said. "If ye're not, ye won't be apprenticing with me. Do ye hear me, girl?" He was near to shouting.

"Good God," his brother grumbled from four feet away. "The dead heard ye in the churchyard and beyond."

Willoughby glared at him.

"Aye. I'll be there," Sophie assured him. "On time, too. Will you excuse us, please?"

She grabbed Hugh's arm and dragged him to the stained-glass window of Saint Columba. "So ye didn't believe me until ye heard it from someone else? Did ye think I'd made everything up? That I had faked the emails?" She lowered her voice to a hiss. "That I'd done it all so I could get into yere bed?"

A harrumph shot up from behind her. She turned to see a sour-faced woman wrapped in a wool coat the same color as sheep dung.

Sophie turned red, but she still had more to say to Hugh, so she pulled him closer. "Believe me...the show yere reflection gave me wasn't worth my time."

The Laird wasn't affected in the least. In fact, he made matters worse by running his hand down her arm like they were lovers. "Darling, don't say such hurtful things. I thought ye liked my naked arse."

The battle-ax's mouth fell open, and she hurried away into the chapel, likely ready to burst with gossip.

"Just like that," Sophie said. "Ye'd ruin yere reputation."

"Aye. Just like that. That old woman is Nansaidh. She's been wanting dirt on me for years because I wouldn't walk out with her granddaughter. I think we're finally even. I've made her happier than the woolgatherer on sheep-shearing day."

Sure enough, Nansaidh was nattering away with woman after woman, pointing to the Laird in the Narthex, most certainly filling their ears full of how the lord of the manor had fallen.

Sophie perched her hands on her hips. "What of my reputation?"

Hugh winked at her. "What's one more naked arse when ye've already seen so many?"

"Ye're insufferable."

He slipped an arm around her and kissed the top of her head.

Sophie couldn't move. She couldn't think. She thought she might melt away right there within the walls of the church.

"Stay at my house and apprentice with Willoughby for the next week," he said into her hair. "If ye can stand him that long."

"How am I going to stand you?"

He laughed and toyed with a lock of her mane. "That's not what we're debating here. What do ye say, lass?"

She leaned back and stared into his clear brown eyes. Eyes that had depth to them. Solid, like oak.

The church door opened, and he dropped the bit of her hair that he held.

The newcomer came straight to them. Sophie knew her— Amy's aunt. Hugh's aunt, too. Aunt Davinia.

"It wouldn't be right to stay with ye at yere house," Sophie said before Aunt Davinia reached them. "Not all alone."

Aunt Davinia gave her a sly smile and then beamed at Hugh. The older woman was aging wonderfully, as Hugh would probably do, too. "What's this all about?" she asked innocently. Aunt Davinia gave Sophie a kiss on the cheek. "It's good to see you again, dear. Now, tell Aunt Davinia why ye're frowning."

Hugh shook his head at his aunt, but Sophie answered her anyway.

"I'm here to apprentice with the kiltmaker. But I thought I would be at Kilheath Castle alone. I'm not the type of lass to plant myself in a man's home, especially one I'm not married to." Besides, as Sophie's parents had made clear—she wasn't marriage material anyway.

Aunt Davinia patted Hugh's arm. "Ye better hold on to this one, laddie. The rest of the world is shacking up at every opportunity." She grabbed Sophie's hand and placed it in Hugh's. "But this lass, my dear boy, has moral fiber."

Sophie was still stuck on her words. Ye better hold on to this one. Then the heat of his hand and the satisfying, steady grip of it made her feel a little dizzy.

Hugh dropped her hand and then wheeled on his relation. "Auntie, ye wouldn't know anything about any emails now, would ye? Or perhaps that my clothes were cleared out of my own dresser drawers and shoved in the back of my closet?"

Aunt Davinia waved him off with a laugh. "Ye've always been one with the outrageous imagination, Hugh-boy. Now, Sophie, not to worry. I recently moved from Fairge to the dower house on the north end of Hugh's property. I would be right happy to move into the big house for the next week to make things proper for you and my nephew."

Hugh studied the statue of Saint Jude, the patron saint of lost causes. "Then I'll have one of the rooms furnished up for ye."

Who was he speaking to? Aunt Davinia? Did he mean for Sophie to sleep in his sister's room? Or with him?

The organist began Pachelbel's Canon in D. Sleeping arrangements would have to wait until after the service.

Aunt Davinia gave Sophie's hand one last squeeze before the older woman hurried into the chapel.

Hugh put his hand to Sophie's back again, but this time leaned down and spoke in her ear. "Ye'll sit in the family pew with us."

The words were innocent, but the thoughts he conjured up weren't. His warm breath on her neck and ear made her a little wobbly on her feet and filled her with—she hated to admit it—desire. The devil.

He grinned at her burning face and then placed a finger on one of her incinerated cheeks. "Do ye need to step outside and cool off first, lass?"

"Nay." She'd just burn in hell for her less-than-pure fanciful thoughts—and in church, no less.

# CHAPTER THREE

Hugh sat through the Sunday service, cognizant of his houseguest next to him. Sophie was as straight as a matchstick. Was she as hyperaware of him as he was of her?

After the service, he hurried out after her, not stopping to speak with the pastor or his workers. He caught up to her just outside the cemetery fence.

"Have ye entered a footrace?" he asked.

She shrugged off the hand he'd put at her back. "Hugh, if I do stay at Kilheath Castle, I won't be staying in your sister's room."

"Are ye wanting mine then?" he said with more than a hint of sarcasm.

"I do love the view."

As far as he was concerned, the view could be dashed. Especially the view of the loch. Too many memories. Too many regrets.

She paused before the first sheepgate. "Nay. I don't want yere room either."

A strange feeling came over him. Disappointment? He chalked it up to being a blasted male with sex always on his mind.

"Maybe I should stay at the dower house," Sophie offered.

"There's no space for ye," Hugh lied. "You'll stay at Kilheath." With me.

"The emails?" she asked, throwing him off guard. "You really think it was Aunt Davinia?"

"Aye, she and Amy must've been in cahoots."

"But why?"

Because he'd stopped living—at least, that's what Auntie and Amy had been saying. Since he'd moved back home and taken over McGillivray's House of Woolens, he'd immersed himself in his work. When his parents had died in the auto crash, he'd lost his last chance to make things right between him and Mum and Da.

"I don't know why Amy and Auntie did it," Hugh lied again. "I'll not let ye go home until ye've learned how to make a kilt to Deydie's satisfaction. Plus, I'll make sure ye have a bushel of woolens for Deydie and her quilting retreat."

Sophie touched his arm, pulling him to a stop. As he looked into her eyes, he seemed to wake up or to come alive again… at least a very little bit. The deadness and coldness that had settled into his chest eased.

"Thank you." She squeezed his arm. "Ye don't know what this means to me."

But he could read the emotions in her eyes. He saw kindness, and trust, and at the place that she tried to hide the most, he saw want and need. Was it for him?

"Come," he said. Enough of these moments. He steered her toward Kilheath. "Let's find a place to settle ye into my home."

Nothing more was said as they walked back. The sky had turned cloudy and gray. Sophie's mood seemed to have darkened with it. The Wallace and the Bruce met them at the door and followed them into the kitchen. Hugh pulled the plate of pork sandwiches from the refrigerator drawer that Mrs. McNabb had left. When they sat down to eat, Sophie was quiet and distant. He started to say something—anything—to cheer her up, when the sun peeked out from the clouds.

She popped up. "I'm taking the dogs for a walk."

"But you haven't even taken a bite."

"I'm not hungry." But she looked at the sandwich like she was.

"I'll go with you," Hugh offered.

"Nay. Stay here. I'll be out of yere hair, and then you can enjoy yere lunch."

But Hugh liked having her around. The thought shocked him.

She reached for the leashes on the hook, and his hounds went nuts, their backsides wagging as if he hadn't just walked them this morning.

She gave the dogs a small smile, a welcome sight after her sullenness of the last half hour or so. "While I'm putting jeans on, can you get the dogs ready? Put their leashes on them?"

"Aye."

"Stay." The dogs plopped their hindquarters down, smiling at her as if she were the master. "You stay, too, Hugh. I'll be in yere room for only a minute."

He watched her go, his tongue hanging out, just like the dogs'. Nothing like being bossed around by a lovely Scottish lass.

Sophie hurried into her jeans, a heavy sweater, and warm boots. The sun could return behind the clouds any second, and she intended to soak up every bit of the natural light while she could. Her therapy lamp did wonders, but real sunlight had a miraculous effect on her mood and well-being. She had felt the doldrums coming on during the church service, and she hoped a few minutes of sunlight would chase them away.

When she got downstairs, Hugh waited at the door. "Are ye sure ye don't want me along?"

"I'm sure."

He handed her the leashes and held the door open for her. "Don't be long. A storm is coming. I don't want to come traipsing after ye in the snow to find ye." He pointed to the dogs. "Those bluidy bastards have no sense of direction, and their sense of smell is worse. Don't rely on them to get you home."

The way he said home made her feel warm and fluttery. Which was ridiculous.

"I'll be grand," she quipped. "I've got my bearings. We're just going out for a wee stroll in the sun."

Hugh looked up. "Then ye better hurry before yere sun goes behind that big cloud over there."

Sophie, the Wallace, and the Bruce set out. She wanted to stay in the wide open, thinking of heading toward the Munro, but a rabbit moved to the right. The dogs took off, pulling Sophie into the dense woods. They may not have good noses, but there was nothing wrong with their eyesight.

As they pulled her deeper into the forest, she called after them to halt, but the dogs ignored her. After a while, they seemed to have lost the trail completely. When she was able to pull them to a stop, she gave them a stern talking-to, and then realized she didn't know which way was back to the house. She turned in a circle. In the clearing beyond sat a large boulder with the sun shining on it. She took the Wallace and the Bruce and perched on the rock. As soon as she shut her eyes and put her face heavenward, the dogs went crazy, jerking the leashes free from her hand.

"Dammit," she yelled. The rabbit had returned, and the dogs were gone.

No amount of hollering and chasing after them made them stop either, or let her catch up to them.

Now what was she to do? She should've thought to stick her phone in her pocket. Or even better, she should've accepted Hugh's offer to come along.

And wouldn't he be angry with her for losing his dogs!

She trudged into the forest in the direction that the ornery buggers had gone, figuring she'd find them first before making her way back to civilization. The dogs' barks became fainter and fainter, until she didn't hear them at all.

That's when snow started to fall.

Hugh stood at the back door, thinking the lass really should have returned by now. The temperature had plummeted, and the air was heavy with moisture. She was a grown woman, not a little girl. But then it started snowing. Hard. He waited ten more minutes—certain she would show herself any second—and willing himself not to be anxious. He had seen her heading toward the Munro, but had forced himself from the window to leave her in peace to walk alone. Thoughts of her stayed behind in the kitchen as if she'd never left him. He wished she hadn't.

"Blast it all!" He grabbed his coat, hat, and gloves and stepped outside. He would ring her neck for making him worry…about his hounds.

He started down the path that led up to the Munro until he heard a noise. He turned and saw the Wallace and the Bruce trotting up to him from the opposite direction, dragging their leashes behind them.

Hugh looked beyond, waiting for Sophie to materialize at the edge of the woods, all the while formulating the lecture he would give her. She didn't appear.

Holy hell. This was why he would never have the responsibility of a family. He'd let his parents down once, and the consequences had been horrific. Images flashed through his brain, but he put them aside.

Where was Sophie? What if she was hurt?

He took off at a run. The dogs thought it was a great game and ran after him. Hugh stopped and grabbed at their leashes, pulling them to him.

"Where is she, lads? Where did ye leave yere lady?" His

voice sounded a little frantic to his own ears.

The Bruce whined, but the Wallace's ear perked up. They were a couple of worthless hounds, but something had gotten into the Wallace.

"Can ye take me to her? Can ye remember where ye left her?" Hugh rubbed his head. "Show me."

The snow was coming down almost sideways now, working itself into a whiteout. He prayed to God that Sophie was okay. And if she wasn't, he was going to kill her!

The dogs led him deep into the woods, and Hugh was starting to worry that he himself might get lost with the weather the way it was. But when they came upon the clearing with the boulder, he knew his exact location. The problem was, he didn't know hers!

A hint of burning wood hit his senses. He looked skyward for smoke but could see only snow. The smoke had to be coming from the crofter's cabin on the other side of the clearing. The cabin that he and Amy had played in as children...their make-believe castle.

He put his head down and started plowing in the direction of the cabin, praying Sophie was there, safe and sound.

As he got close, the dogs began barking and dragging him along. When he stepped onto the porch, the door flew open, and the dogs barreled past her, leaving a shocked and relieved Sophie in their wake.

He stepped in and slammed the door behind him. "Thank God! You worried the hell out me!"

"Hugh," she said on a breath.

He didn't think—he couldn't, his relief was so great. He tracked her down, like an animal on the scent, leaned her up against the wall, and kissed her, punishing her—most specifically her lips—for upsetting him.

Kissing calmed him. Soothed him. Made him harder than the boulder in the clearing.

He was covered in snow from head to foot, but Sophie

wrapped her arms around his cold body anyway and kissed him back—hard.

"God, Sophie," he growled as he pulled away, but only far enough to tug at the neck of her sweater so he could kiss her there. "Why would ye do that to me, lass?"

She moaned, dropping her head to the side as he kissed the base of her throat. "I got lost."

He looked into her eyes. "Don't do it again."

"Don't kiss you again?"

"No." He chuckled. "I'm not daft." He liked that he could kiss her until she was foggy. He pushed her blond hair back from her face and gave her one more quick kiss on the lips.

Things started registering around him. The smell of bacon reached his nose. No, canned ham. She'd made use of the provisions that he kept at these outlying crofters' cottages.

His clothes were wet, and he'd soaked her while forcing his torrid kisses on her. But she'd kissed him back!

The Bruce and the Wallace had stretched out on the twin bed, making themselves at home, soaking it as well.

"Down, ye fools," he growled at them.

They slunk off the bed.

Sophie stared at the bed, too. Was she also imagining what she and Hugh might do there? He sure as hell was!

Maybe it was just as well that the hounds had ruined the bedding. Hugh wouldn't make Sophie lie on a damp bed while he drove himself into her.

"The food smells good," he said awkwardly. He stood by the fire, his clothes and boots dripping all over the floor.

"Get out of yere things," she said matter-of-factly. "Ye'll catch yere death. I'll make ye a cup of tea."

He wondered irrationally if she wanted him to strip down to his nothings, how she'd seen him last night in his bedroom. Nah, probably not.

"There should be whisky here somewhere." He shrugged off his snow-covered coat and hung it on the back of the chair. He dragged the chair in front of the fire.

The cabin was small with the four of them in the one room. The more he stared at Sophie, the less he could breathe. At the same time, all her bustling around and taking care of things made it all seem pretty damn cozy.

As Sophie made a plate of ham and beans, the Wallace and the Bruce put their noses in the air, sniffing.

"It's not for ye." Though the Wallace had known where to find her. "Come here, boy." Hugh dug in his pocket and pulled out a dog biscuit, patting the dog firmly when he came to get his treat. "Ye did good."

Because the Bruce never missed out on a treat, he nosed his way between them, and he got a biscuit, too.

"Come sit at the table," Sophie ordered with her still-swollen lips. As if for proof, she put a finger to the bottom one, rubbing it.

"Let me get the dogs' food first," Hugh said. "I've got a container under the counter."

He had to pass by her on his way. It took everything in him not to pull her into his arms again…and maybe not stop this time.

After he took care of the dogs, he joined her by the hearth, taking a bite of ham. He was warming up and couldn't completely credit the fire.

"You scared the shite out of me," he said as way of conversation. Better to be angry than to be drawn to her. "Why would ye head off into the woods?"

"Like I had a choice in the matter." She nodded to his hounds. "Yere beasts saw a rabbit they took a liking to."

"Well, ye should've agreed to have me come along."

"Aye." She poked the fire like she didn't want to meet his eyes. "Hugh? Last summer, why wouldn't ye dance with me at the céilidh? Why did ye ignore me so thoroughly?"

The question caught him off guard. But turnabout was fair play. He'd caught her off guard when he'd kissed her a bit ago. He'd like to do it again. Instead, he faced her, the firelight catching the blue of her eyes. He could make out the old hurt in the depths of them, and he felt bad for it.

He pushed back her hair and hoped she could see the earnestness of what he felt. "Aw, lass, last summer, didn't ye know? Ye took my breath away. But my life wasn't my own. It still isn't. My parents had died in the crash a month before, and I had only just moved home to take over the wool business. I was half-dead inside, and ye had too much life for me."

Aye, even now.

She laid a hand on his arm, as if steadying him. "I'm going to finish eating, and then I have to get back to the big house."

She'd knocked him off-balance again with her statement… another non sequitur.

"Sophie, we can't go anywhere. It's a blizzard. We'll have to wait out the storm." Couldn't she see that? "Tomorrow morning will be soon enough. We'll need the light to see our way home."

She pulled back the curtain and gazed outside. "You don't understand. I need the light now."

He placed a hand on her shoulder. "We have the fire. There should be a torch or two somewhere and new batteries in the cabinet. I know there are candles. We'll have enough light." Was she as scared of the dark as he'd been as a child? "Ye're safe with me, lass."

"Ye're not the problem." She yanked the damp quilt off the bed and hung it over the second chair back. "I am."

"What?" Hugh looked at Sophie as if she'd gone mental.

Which was pretty spot-on. How could she tell Hugh about her disorder? She liked him. If she was being honest with herself—which she wasn't—she liked him a lot, and had since the moment she'd laid eyes on him last June. She was being ridiculous. She didn't have a future with Hugh, or with any other man, for that matter. Her spinster status had been a foregone conclusion ages ago. Summer Sophie had dated, but nothing ever lasted as Dead-of-Winter Sophie surfaced in early fall. She'd known her whole life that she'd never be able to marry. She was too messed up to have a relationship. Then her parents confirmed it—too old and bossy—unmarriageable.

"Take me back to the house," she commanded. "Please."

"I don't understand what's going on here. There's nothing wrong with ye," he argued.

For a second, hope flickered inside her that Hugh was blind to her disorder. But it wouldn't do any good if he was. He'd made it clear that he was too busy to be in a relationship. Or maybe he had been making it clear that he didn't want to be in a relationship with her!

It didn't matter. Emma would tell her to be honest. Own her disorder and not be ashamed of it.

Sophie squared her shoulders and looked him in the eye—the best that she could—by cranking her head back.

"You met me in the summer, Hugh, when, yes, I'm full of life." She motioned to the world beyond the cabin. "But we're in the dead of winter now, when, I assure ye, things can be quite the opposite."

"What are ye talking about?" He scanned her from head to toe. "Ye look fine to me. Ye're not sick, are ye?"

"Aye. In a manner of speaking."

She told him all about her disorder. How overwhelming and hopeless life became. How listless she felt. How dressing, hygiene, and proper nutrition became nearly impossible. How even the simple task of getting out of bed didn't seem feasible during the long winter months.

"Ye see, I have to get back to the house," she said, finishing. "I need my light, or I might step back into the darkness."

He took her hand and squeezed. "I told ye, lass, that ye're safe with me. I'll be here to help ye find yere way."

She stepped from him, embarrassed. He was sweet for offering to see her through the sadness, and for a second, she almost believed him. But he was perfect and she was damaged. The hurt bubbled up. "I may've shared my deepest, darkest secret with ye, but I'll not let ye witness Dead-of-Winter Sophie." He had pity in his eyes, which only infuriated her. "You and yere perfect six-foot-three, world-traveling, castle-owning and keeper of two lovable dogs self can't possibly know what it's like for me." She thought about the small cottage she shared with her parents in Gandiegow. About how her disorder would keep her from having even their small town happiness, from getting married, from having a family to call her own. "Ye can't possibly know," she repeated sharply.

He grabbed her shoulders. "So ye've cornered the market on pain and suffering."

Because Sophie didn't know why he was so mad, and she was already feeling pretty crappy and irrational, she stood up to him. "What do you know about not being able to drag yereself out of bed? Or about not having enough energy to care about anything or anybody?" Her voice cracked, but she finished. "Ye can't possibly understand."

"Ye're not the only one who is well acquainted with the darker side of life."

"Really?" she said sarcastically.

He gave her shoulders a firm shake. "Do you know what it feels like to be afraid to go to sleep at night? To be so afraid of the dark that ye want to howl at the moon?" He shook her again.

"But ye're so successful." So together. So Hugh.

"Come." He pulled the quilt from the chair back as he tugged her toward the bed.

"Whoa. I'm not that kind of girl—I'm not easy." Though she was pretty sure that it wouldn't take many more of his sweltering kisses to change her mind.

"Sit."

The Wallace and the Bruce looked like the master had lost it.

She pulled free. "Do I look like one of yere pets?"

"Sorry. I've been alone with the dogs for too long. Please sit beside me."

Hugh spread the quilt on the bed. "It's all dry now." He glanced at his dogs. "No thanks to you two."

He positioned himself with his back against the wall and patted the spot next to him. "Take a load off, Sophie."

She looked at him skeptically.

"I promise—hands to myself."

"Fine. I'll sit, but only if ye talk to me. I mean, really talk to me. Why would ye ever want to howl at the moon?"

He shook his head.

She folded her arms over her chest, prepared to stand there for the long haul. "Fair's fair, Hugh. I told ye all about me. Now it's your turn."

He sighed resignedly. "I'll only tell ye so you won't feel like ye're the only one who's experienced misery."

She slid in beside him.

He sat silent for so long that she began to wonder if he would speak at all. Finally, he took her hand and looked off into the distance—beyond the wall where the dishes were stacked on the shelf. "As I said…I'm afraid of the dark."

He wore an expression of complete sincerity and seriousness.

He shrugged. "I know it's ridiculous, but it's true. It all started after my sister, well, after her accident."

As encouragement, she rested her other hand over his. "Go on."

"I was eleven when she had her accident. She was a wee bit, only five. I was supposed to be watching her as we played by the loch's edge. Da had warned us about not going out on the loch, as the ice had thinned. Chrissa and I were building a fort out of the new snow. She got bored and wanted to go inside, but I made her stay with me. Mum and Da were busy with the wool mill. I became so entranced with my work of building the fort that I forgot all about her. Until I heard the ice cracking." He winced like he was experiencing it all over again. "I looked up just in time to see her fall through."

"Oh, Hugh." Sophie laid her head on his shoulder, trying to comfort him.

"I didn't even think—I ran out after her. I weighed much more, and the ice gave way underneath me sooner. As I fell in, I kept my eyes on where she'd gone in, but she never came back up, not even once. I was determined to save her and ignored the cold. I put my head in the water and opened my eyes. I thought if I could see her, I could get to her. But I only saw black. No Chrissa, only murky, dark water." He shifted away. "I failed. I was going to join her. Lethargy had set in, and I knew I wouldn't be able to get myself out either."

He paused for a long moment. "My da had seen me from the window, the cook told me later. He hadn't seen Chrissa. He yanked me from the loch, giving me a bluidy lecture the whole time for going out on the loch when told not to. When I finally said Chrissa's name and pointed, the lecture stopped. It was as if my da died, too. Mum, also. The life left them, and I became afraid of the dark."

Hugh's breathing had become shallow. Sophie bit her lower lip to keep herself from sobbing.

He went on as if he had no choice. "At night, when I shut my eyes, I see Chrissa lost in the murky black waters of the loch. When I sleep, the dark waters haunt me. Did I tell ye I have nightmares, every night?" He looked in her eyes for the answer. "No, of course not. I'm cursed with the bluidy things, but I have taught myself to rein in my fear of the dark. Ye asked me why I dinna turn on the light when coming to bed…it's what I do to show myself that my fear hasn't owned me. I can't stop the nightmares. But I am managing the dark." He raised Sophie's hand to his lips and kissed the back of it. "Now ye know my darkest secret. Ye see, lass, ye're not alone in yere pain."

She shifted toward him and laid her free hand on his cheek, looking into his eyes with her misty ones. "And ye're not alone in yeres."

"I've never talked about it with another soul. Not Amy and not my aunt either."

To have lost a loved one in such a way and to be so tortured tore at Sophie's heart. In a moment of compassion and bravery, she pulled him to her for a tender kiss, giving the light within her to comfort him. She held him tight, willing his pain to be eased. After a moment, she could feel his burden lift a little, and something shifted between them. The kiss became heated—a veritable fire had broken out—and Sophie was comforting Hugh no longer.

She was doing this for herself. She needed Hugh, and she kissed him passionately to let him know how she felt.

So what if her parents said that she'd never find a man? So what if she never had one that would be hers for always? She didn't want to be a virgin for always either. Maybe—just maybe—she could have this man for tonight.

# CHAPTER FOUR

Hugh lost himself in Sophie's kiss—in her goodness, in her light, in her comfort. She handed it all to him with the touch of her lips…he was overwhelmed. Until he realized what she was doing—unbuttoning his shirt. And what he was doing—trying to unzip her jeans.

"Enough," he growled more to himself than to her. He pulled away. He hadn't told her his story so he could get down to her intriguing underthings!

"I'm sorry." She looked stricken.

Oh, God! He wrapped his arms around her, speaking into her hair. "Ye're not the kind of lass who would let a bastard like me seduce ye," he said thickly. "Let me hold ye, and let's see if we both can get through this night undamaged."

The dogs came over and plopped themselves close to the bed in a show of solidarity.

"Okay," she said on a sniffle.

Dammit. He rubbed her arms, and she shivered. "I'm sorry I made ye cry."

"Ye didn't," she said. "It's just talking about making it through the night undamaged…it's too late. I'm already damaged, and there's nothing anyone can do about it."

"What are ye talking about, lass?" Had someone physically hurt her?

"It's this disorder. I'll never have the life that I dreamed of. I'll never be like the other women in the village."

He gave her a gentle squeeze. "I don't believe that for a second. Now come, let's see if we can find the cards I stowed here. We could play a game to while away the time."

Her hand drifted over his chest in an absent-minded caress, threatening his few remaining wits.

"What if I told you, Hugh, that kissing you makes me happy? That yere kisses are as good as lying under a thousand suns?"

Sophie Munro was a minx. No two ways about it.

He pushed her up from the bed, swatting her bottom gently in the process. "I'd say, I think ye're testing me, lass. Play some cards with me. I promise, if I see ye're succumbing to sadness, I'll kiss ye." And the devil take him, too.

While they sat at the table, playing high-stakes poker with matchsticks, Hugh entertained Sophie with stories of the shenanigans that he and Amy had gotten up to as children. He admitted that he'd had a hard time at first being taken from his home to Aunt Davinia's, because her house had been so lively. Amy was legendary for her nonstop talking. He'd soon settled in at his aunt's, deciding he had the better of it to be away from Kilheath Castle and the constant reminder of the loss of his sister.

After a while, the dogs needed to go outside. Hugh took them, but when he returned, Sophie didn't seem as cheerful as when he'd left.

"How are ye feeling?"

She shrugged.

"Come here, lass."

She stepped into his arms, and he held her.

"Will ye kiss me, Hugh? For the sake of releasing some endorphins?"

"Ye're such a romantic, Sophie Munro."

"Will ye?"

"I promised, didn't I?" He leaned down and kissed her. He meant to be tender and gentle, but she felt so damn good that he let himself go. When her knees buckled, he scooped her into his arms and carried her to the bed. He wouldn't make love to her, but he would do his best to make her feel better.

Before he laid her on the mattress, though, the door flew open. Belatedly, the hounds barked. Sophie squeaked. She tried to wiggle out of his arms, but Hugh held her tighter. Three people rushed in, shaking the snow off their coats and stomping their snow-covered boots all over the cabin floor.

The shorter and oldest of them moved forward, while pushing back the hood of her mackinaw.

"Aunt Davinia?" Hugh gently set Sophie on her feet. "What in the deuce are ye doing here?"

"I thought we were here to save you. We brought both ATVs."

Donal and Fergus, his gardener and his ghillie, stood behind the matriarch, not making eye contact and looking ruddy in the face. Hugh didn't care—they were both fired!

Sophie tiptoed behind him to the hearth and busied herself with bolstering the fire.

"Who said that I needed saving?" Hugh asked his meddling aunt.

She raised an eyebrow at him, something she'd perfected when he was a boy. "From what I'm seeing, I've seriously misjudged the situation." She frowned like she wanted to back out of the door and let them get back to it.

"Oh, good grief! Nothing inappropriate happened." Except if they'd arrived five minutes later, it might have. "Sophie got lost in the woods," Hugh explained. "The Wallace and the Bruce led me here to find her. We thought the weather was too bad to make a go of it on foot tonight."

"Nicely recapped," Auntie said, taking his arm. "Leaving

out all the best parts, I see." She leaned in, whispering conspiratorially, "If ye'd only let me know where ye were and what ye're doing, I would've given ye my blessing." She smiled over at Sophie, then put her focus back on him. "She's a dear." She shook his arm then. "But ye didn't, and ye weren't answering yere mobile. I assumed the worst."

"Then how did you find me?"

"I GPS'ed your phone, darling," making it sound innocent and normal that an elderly aunt knew how to hack a computer.

"I had my phone silenced for church," Hugh explained, wishing he'd remembered to unmute it. What he didn't explain was that since Sophie had stepped into his life…he'd become distracted.

He ran a hand through his hair, deciding his aunt's arrival was for the best. "Sophie, get yere coat. Ye're going home."

Sophie gasped as if he'd jabbed her with a hot poker.

"To Kilheath. Home to Kilheath Castle," he clarified.

"Oh." She frowned at the roaring fire. "But I just stoked it."

Hugh had to agree. She had stoked the flame between them as well, and it would take some time to douse what she'd started.

"Donal, take Miss Munro back with you." Donal seemed the better choice—married to a lovely woman and in his fifties. Fergus, though, was known as somewhat of a ladies' man. "Then come back to get me. I'll stay and put out the fire."

Donal nodded. "Miss, if ye're ready."

Sophie grabbed her coat, not looking at Hugh as she slipped it on. But Hugh saw her red cheeks, which had nothing to do with the fire in the hearth. She looked hell-bent to get out of there.

But he was a bastard.

"Wait up a minute," he said. He retrieved her hat from the table and went to her, leaning over, speaking so quietly that only she could hear. "We'll talk when I get home. There's still the matter of where ye're going to sleep tonight."

— ✦ —

Sophie didn't need her coat on her way back to Kilheath Castle. Aye, it was still snowing out. Aye, she should've been a Sophie Popsicle riding on the back of the ATV with Donal. But she was so heated up by Hugh's closeness back at the cottage, not to mention his double entendre that she was downright smoldering. And she should be ashamed of herself for not feeling bad about it.

She was quite flattered by Hugh's attention, but she couldn't possibly think it meant anything. To be stuck out in the countryside with so few prospects of female companionship had to be awful for him. Before moving back to Lalkanbroch village, Hugh had lived in Edinburgh, a different girl every night, according to Amy. He was simply hard up…which explained his attention to Sophie tonight. Lucky for her, the wool mill was out in the middle of nowhere.

Donal pulled the ATV to the back door and stopped.

"Thank you for the ride back." Sophie climbed off the vehicle, looking toward the woods as if Hugh might magically appear.

"Don't worry, miss, I'll get the Laird now."

She started to argue with Donal that she wasn't worried about anyone, but the man had taken off already.

Sophie hurried into the mudroom, stripping off her snow-covered coat and kicking off her boots. She wanted to be changed into dry clothes and her things cleared from his room before the Laird returned.

She hustled her way through the house, hearing Aunt Davinia come in the back door as well. Sophie didn't stop, climbing the two flights of stairs quickly. She knew she was being ridiculous, but she wanted to be back in the kitchen sipping tea when the master arrived home.

And she wanted to be composed…which she wasn't sure she could pull off just yet.

She peeled off her clothes and put on dry ones, a delayed chill setting in. Or was it nerves? As she opened Hugh's top dresser drawer to unload it, there was a knock at the door.

He can't be home already!

"Let me in, dear." Only Aunt Davinia.

Before Sophie answered the door, she closed Hugh's drawer, not wanting Davinia to glimpse her underthings.

Aunt Davinia pulled her out into the hallway. "Come downstairs and have a cuppa with me."

"No, thank you." Sophie's things were strewn about Hugh's bedroom. "I best clean this up."

Aunt Davinia shuffled her farther into the hall, reaching in to close the door. "You can take care of that later."

"But—"

The older woman looped her arm through hers. "Don't argue with Aunt Davinia. You need to warm yere bones."

Sophie allowed herself to be led down the stairs and back to the kitchen. Just as they got settled at the table, the door opened and the dogs rushed in, shaking snow from their massive bodies. Hugh appeared next, windblown, his cheeks alive from the brutal weather, and looking absolutely gorgeous.

Aunt Davinia grabbed another mug, filled it with tea, and thrust it into his hands. "Take Sophie into the parlor, Hugh-boy, and warm her up in front of the fire."

Hugh gave his aunt a pointed look.

"Run along now," the old woman said, while blowing on her tea. "When Auntie is around, ye have to do as she bids."

He sighed as if Sophie was a burden. Was it so terrible that he should sit in the parlor with her? He hadn't thought she was such an inconvenience when they'd been kissing awhile ago.

Sophie picked up her mug, hugging it to her body, and huffed from the room.

Hugh was right behind her.

She should go back to his room, pack up her things, and find a corner of the house to call her own tonight. Then tomorrow, she would check around to see if she could stay anyplace other than Kilheath Castle. She certainly didn't want to put the Laird out!

Sophie marched straight to the parlor's fire, keeping her back to Hugh. She spun around when she heard the pocket doors being pulled closed.

"What are ye doing?"

He stalked toward her, stopping directly in front of her. "Remember? Our private chat?"

Did he mean to pick up where he'd left off with her lips? Her middle warmed, and it had nothing to do with the fire.

She turned around. "I won't be a burden. I'll only stay the night, then tomorrow I'll find somewhere else to stay while I apprentice with Mr. Willoughby."

"Masterson."

"What?"

"Willoughby Masterson." Hugh ran a lock of Sophie's hair between his fingers.

"Oh," she said breathlessly.

"Ye're not a burden."

Heat rolled off of him. Her insides were melting, and for a moment, she forgot to be mad at him for treating her like a liability. Instead, she wanted to stand closer to soak him in.

"What did ye want to talk about?" She was out of oxygen.

He looked ready to lean in and take possession of her lips, body, and soul. Sophie came to her senses just in time and moved away.

Hugh stepped closer. "Ye'll sleep in my room tonight."

She opened her mouth to protest, but he put his hand up.

"Don't argue. I'm the Laird."

"Aye. Ye're the Laird," she agreed. "But this isn't some scene from Outlander. Ye can't order me around."

"Sophie, it's the only thing to do. Ye were brought here under false pretenses. Let me fix it."

She studied him for a long moment. He was a decent man

who wanted to make things right. Perhaps he didn't see her as a burden after all. She longed to cuddle up to him, to be a comfort. She had her bright-light therapy to help her. What did he have to help him? "What about you?"

"I'll sleep elsewhere." Though his eyes showed more than a hint of disappointment.

If they were still back at the cabin and Aunt Davinia hadn't come to rescue them, Sophie would probably be in Hugh's arms right now, naked, finding out what it was like to be with a man. She fanned herself.

Then she remembered the predicament of where he would bed down for the night. "Where exactly will you sleep?" The loveseat in front of the fire hadn't been all that comfortable last night and she was much shorter than Hugh. "You yereself said that the other rooms weren't made up." That meant that, for tonight, Aunt Davinia wouldn't be in the house either.

"I'll take my sister's room."

"No, you can't."

"I can." Hugh grabbed her hands. "After Chrissa died, I slept on her floor every night until Aunt Davinia came and took me away."

Sophie got the feeling that occupying his sister's room was something Hugh needed to do, and maybe he knew it subconsciously, too. Perhaps sleeping beside his dead sister's bed would help heal him. She wondered what Emma would think about his plan. Would this be therapy for him, like her lamp was for her?

Either way, Sophie could do something for him now. She wrapped comforting arms around him and came to a decision…he wouldn't have to do this alone. She would be there for him, no matter what. She would sleep on the floor beside him tonight.

— ⁓◦◦◦⁓ —

Hugh liked Sophie's arms around him—verra much. He liked that she rubbed circles into his back. He liked the warmth of her buried into his chest. He tipped her head back and kissed her, showing her how much he liked…her. She snaked her arms around his neck. She must like him a little, too.

As he laid her back on the sofa, she made a soft hmmm sound. When he tried to pull away to make sure everything was okay, she tightened her arms around his neck. He ran his hand down the length of her and found the hem of her sweater. Just as he was exploring under her top, searching for skin, the pocket doors opened.

Sophie tried to scramble away from underneath him. He stilled her with his gaze while removing his hands where they shouldn't have been.

"Hugh? Darling?" Aunt Davinia walked farther into the room.

They both sat up—Hugh still held on to Sophie.

"Oh, yes." His aunt pretended to be embarrassed by the debauchery in the parlor. "I see you were telling yere guest good night."

Hugh sighed heavily. "Yes, Auntie? What do ye need?"

"Donal is going to run me back to the dower house for tonight. But, darling, please don't forget to feed yere guest. I believe she's going to need her strength."

Sophie, red-faced, slipped off the couch and went to the writing desk in the corner. A rectangular lamp sat on top. She grabbed a book, sat down, and turned on the lamp.

"Good night, dear." Aunt Davinia, who didn't seem at all surprised to see Sophie in front of the bright light, waved to her.

Sophie glanced up for only a second. "Night, Aunt Davinia."

Hugh should've felt bad for accosting Sophie a moment ago, but he couldn't work up any regret. He wanted to go back to her, rub her back, fondle her hair, or something. He needed to keep touching her, but instead he followed Davinia into the hallway.

"Auntie?" he called.

"Yes, Hugh-boy. What is it?"

"I need to know something. Is there anything else that ye've done? Tell me now if ye and Amy are done conniving."

Aunt Davinia laughed heartily and walked away.

Sophie had her eyes glued to some book, but her focus was all on the Laird when he came back into the parlor. He went to a stack of magazines, grabbed one, and stretched out on the loveseat, his legs hanging off. The air was rife with sexual tension, or with Sophie's wishful thinking; it was hard to tell which.

The Wallace and the Bruce wandered into the room and took up residence at her feet. Those two dogs knew a lot about how to keep a lass company. Sophie planned to talk to Emma about dogs, wondering if they had the therapeutic qualities that she suspected they had. And maybe ask Emma about kissing. Between the hounds at her feet and Hugh's expert lips, Sophie had been doing remarkably well without her therapy lamp all day.

After a while, Hugh left the room and came back with a tray. He didn't say a word, but set a bowl of leftover soup in front of her, soda bread, and a cup of choco, acting like he didn't want to disturb her reading. He ate in front of the fire with the Bruce and the Wallace staring at him—the beggars.

The soup, the warm parlor, and the comfortable companionship made Sophie feel at home. She yawned as Hugh cleared her bowl and spoon from the writing desk.

"What say ye, lass? Are ye ready for bed? It's been a long day."

"Aye." She switched off her lamp. "I believe my lovely trek through the woods has worn me out."

"Come then." He offered his hand. "Let's get you off to bed."

As she placed her hand in Hugh's, she wondered if he

would kiss her good night.

Side by side, they walked up the wide staircase together with the Bruce and the Wallace right on their trail. He didn't stop at his sister's door, but followed her into his room. The dogs jumped on the bed and curled up on either end.

Sophie had forgotten about her clothes strewn all over his floor. While she scooped them up, Hugh closed the door. Had he changed his mind about where he was going to sleep? Her stomach came alive with butterflies doing cartwheels. She waited to see if he would pull her into his arms. But he went to his closet, dug around in the bottom, and retrieved blue plaid pajama bottoms.

Oh. But she still had hope. There was still time for him to make some kind of overture.

Instead, he walked to the door. He hesitated as he exited, but didn't look up. "Good night, Sophie." He closed the door behind him.

She felt stupid for thinking he might try to seduce her. She felt even stupider for still hugging her dirty clothes. Damn him! She threw her bundle at the hard oak door. The Wallace and the Bruce frowned at her...or at least that's what it looked like.

Well, Hugh may not want to crawl into bed with her...and he may have decided on no more kisses, but he sure as hell wasn't going to keep Sophie Munro from sleeping with the Laird tonight.

# CHAPTER FIVE

Hugh changed in the loo down the hall and went back to Chrissa's room. He stood in the doorway for a long moment. He didn't know what had possessed him to give up his own bed and say he would sleep in here. Like a warrior going to battle, he heaved himself over the threshold, shut himself in, and went to Chrissa's closet. He pulled down the stack of quilts that he'd slept on as a grieving lad and made himself a pallet. He didn't want to stop to examine his feelings. He was a grown man now, and he could do this. He shut out the light and lay on the floor next to his dead sister's bed.

He stretched out, looking up at the dark ceiling for a long time, pretty sure that falling asleep would be a futile exercise. He should go downstairs and have a whisky. He could sleep on the damned loveseat like Sophie had done last night. He rolled onto his side.

As if he'd conjured Sophie up, the bedroom door opened and then quietly shut. She tiptoed toward him and softly felt the outline of his back. He didn't speak, anticipating what she would do next, but he got it wrong. She lay down behind him, wrapped one arm around his middle, and curled into his back.

The spoon.

Hugh let out the breath he'd been holding. The spoon grabbed the top quilt and hogged the blankets. He laid his hand over hers, squeezed it, and fell fast asleep in her comforting embrace.

Sophie woke in the morning, sandwiched between two warm bodies—neither of the bodies were Hugh. His dogs were cuddling her. They must've grabbed their chance when Hugh had gotten up. She couldn't blame the hounds. She'd been pretty brazen herself, having the audacity last night to snuggle up to the Laird.

She wasn't sure he even knew she'd been there. He'd never said a word, but had held her in his sleep while she held him. Even though she'd slept on the floor, she felt rested this morning, thoroughly snuggled, like a well-loved quilt. She stretched, rolled over, and threw her arm over—she had to glance up to see—the Wallace. Neither dog budged. A pair of black hiking boots appeared in her lazy-morning line of sight.

The boots' owner cleared his throat.

She glanced up and saw a kilt—rust-colored with green and blue lines. If the Wallace weren't dead to the world, she'd be able to scoot closer to peer underneath. It would serve the Laird right. He'd tried to cop a feel under her sweater last night. Not that she was complaining or anything.

"Are ye going to lie in all day or are ye going to hurry off to the wool mill before Willoughby locks ye out of his workroom?"

"He wouldn't dare," she said. "I have connections. I know the Laird." She cranked her head a little more to the side, but still couldn't be sure what—if anything—he had on under there.

"Well, lass, now that's where ye're wrong. Willoughby told me not thirty minutes ago that if ye weren't there soon, ye'd be shite out of luck. I may be the Laird of this clan and owner of the wool factory, but Willoughby carries the keys to his own workroom."

"Damn." She shoved at the Wallace, but made no headway, getting only a doggie grunt from him.

"Wallace, move," the master said.

The Wallace slowly rose, took two steps, and collapsed. But it was enough room for Sophie to get to her feet.

She gave the Laird the once-over and then whistled through her teeth. "Why're ye wearing yere colors?"

"It's what I wear to the mill." He tapped his watch. "You have ten minutes, if ye plan to be working there today, too."

She hurried past Hugh. "Fine. Will you drive me? So I won't be late?"

"I'll be waiting downstairs."

Sophie put on a white sweater with her Munro tartan skirt. When she got to the kitchen, Hugh had a cup of tea waiting and a bag in his hand.

"It's yere breakfast. Mrs. McNabb will bring our lunch to us later."

"Thank you." She took the sack and hurried out the door to his Mercedes SUV as the sun was peeking over the horizon.

Hugh drove her to the wool mill while she inhaled her cinnamon raisin scone and scalded her mouth on the tea.

"It's delicious," she said around a bite.

Hugh only nodded. He didn't mention last night, and she didn't either. He pulled up to the building farthest from the road.

"He's in there. If he hasn't locked the door already." Hugh had laughter in his voice, but he gave her an encouraging smile. "Go on now. I'll stop by with yere lunch later. Ye can tell me how it goes."

"Thanks again," she said, feeling reluctant to leave his smile, but pulling herself from the car.

"Sophie?"

"Yes?"

"Good luck!" With his eyes dancing, he toasted her with

his travel mug.

Sophie ran inside and met Willoughby at the door. Sure enough, he had the key in his hand, ready to lock her out.

"Ye're late," the old man said.

"No. I'm right on time."

"Well, I didn't think ye'd make it." He sounded disappointed. "I've a lot of work to do. Don't have time for the likes of ye."

Why hadn't she brought an extra scone—some little thing with which to butter up the old man?

"Well, I'm here," she said cheerily. "Ready to make my first kilt."

"Not so fast," Willoughby said. "I'll have to see some of your handiwork first before I'll let ye be touching the tartans with the scissors." With a gnarled hand, he pocketed the key in his old tweed jacket. From inside the coat, he withdrew a thick piece of wool tartan and a needle. He thrust them at her. "Make three evenly spaced pleats."

Sophie claimed a small table and plain ladder-back chair for herself. Willoughby shuffled over to a narrow table that had to be fifteen to twenty feet long. A large bolt of a dark green tartan with a muted aqua blue and royal blue sat at one end.

"Stop staring at me and get busy," he grumbled.

"Aye." What a cheery instructor.

Sophie laid out her length of fabric on the table and grabbed the pins off the windowsill. She went to work, marking evenly spaced pleats and sewing them into place. She should've asked Hugh this morning if he'd strip out of his kilt so she could check to see how the stitching was done.

She smiled at the image and let her mind wander. How nice it'd been sleeping with Hugh last night. And before that, his nakedness in the reflection of his picture windows had been pretty wonderful, too.

Willoughby coughed. "Are ye done yet? We don't have all day."

Sophie walked her pleats over to him. He scowled at her

as he snatched the fabric away, but his expression changed to confusion as he examined the woolen.

"That don't mean a thing," he muttered to himself, shoving the pleated piece back in his inside pocket. "Get up here and start rolling out the tartan. The Laird needs a new kilt. And ye're going to make it." He said it like that would show the new master for off-loading her onto him.

No! She wanted to protest. She didn't trust that her first kilt would be good enough for Hugh. What if she screwed it up?

But if she backed down from this order, Willoughby would throw her out of his workshop for good.

"Fine." She stepped up to the counter. "Eight yards, right?" She began spreading out the wool, wondering if Willoughby was impressed that she knew how much fabric was in a kilt. "I assume this is the McGillivray Hunting tartan."

"Aye." He pointed to a corner where bolts had been stacked. "The modern McGillivray Hunting tartan," Willoughby corrected. "Magnus, me brother, finished weaving it yesterday."

She ran her hand over the quality wool. "It's beautiful."

"I'm glad ye can appreciate craftsmanship. My brother may be an arse, but he does weave the finest tartan in all of Scotland."

His voice held pride, and as he instructed her on how to measure and mark the pleats, his voice became less rough, and she heard the passion for his craft in his words.

At noon, Hugh knocked on the jamb, making Sophie and Willoughby look up from their work.

"Lunch," he said. "Willoughby, do ye want to join us?"

"Nay. I have to complete all the things yere lass kept me from this morning."

Sophie ignored that the old man had lumped her and Hugh together with his yere lass.

"I'll be back soon," she said.

"Don't hurry," Willoughby answered gruffly. He didn't really look angry with her, now that she was getting to know him.

Hugh grabbed her coat and helped her into it. Sophie savored his closeness, allowing a second to breathe him in. She could pretend for this moment that she was his lass, couldn't she?

He walked her out, and as they made their way through the compound, he pointed out the various buildings of the wool operation, starting with the exhibition hall.

"We're a sheep-to-shawl operation," he said proudly. "We do sheep-shearing demonstrations here, but mostly the shearing is done at my cousin Ewan's sheep farm down the way."

"Nepotism?" she kidded.

"Aye, I'm happy to say. Most of our families have been here in the village of Lalkanbroch and have been working at McGillivray's House of Woolens from the beginning. And will continue to be here for generations to come, if I have any say about it."

"What about outsiders? Do ye welcome them?" Sophie's village of Gandiegow could be pretty closed-minded when it came to outsiders moving in.

"Absolutely. We're expanding things here. I have visions of Lalkanbroch becoming an artisan community. I've been working to bring in a potter to set up shop here." He pointed to a funny little green building among the stone cottages. "After that, I'd like to see about getting a basket-maker and an artist here as well."

They passed the building with the waterwheel, and he explained how it provided only a fraction of the energy needed. "We rely mostly on conventional electricity. Though, I strive to keep the old ways alive as much as possible. My father and mother worked hard to preserve the Victorian-era wool mill operation, maintain its authenticity. I'm trying to carry on the tradition. That doesn't mean that some modernization hasn't had to take place. We still have to compete to sell our woolens."

They toured several buildings, and Sophie couldn't help but revel when he'd lay his hand at the small of her back and guided her along. Everyplace they went, the Laird gave her a thorough explanation of each process. He was passionate about what he did, and she couldn't imagine that he'd spent so many years away—or that now that he was home that he would ever leave this place again.

They finally made it to his office in the middle of the complex. Once inside, Hugh settled them at a small conference table in the corner, pulling up two chairs. Sophie retrieved warm meat pies and tea from a picnic basket.

"Compliments of Mrs. McNabb," he said.

Would he bring up last night now? Would he at least bring up how the other bedrooms in the house were coming along? She opened her mouth to ask about the sleeping arrangements, but he jumped in first.

"How are ye getting along with Willoughby?" Hugh asked. "I think he's taken quite a shine to you."

She gave him a half frown. "That's a shine?"

"Aye. He actually let ye stay in his workshop, for one thing. It took Mrs. Bates two years to pass his pleat test before he'd let her sew the buckles on his completed kilts. His damned pleat test is the reason I haven't been able to hire someone to take over…someday."

Sophie was getting a clue as to why Willoughby would be reticent to have her or anyone else there. He saw her as a threat. She'd have to assure him that she had no intention of taking his place. She was going home soon.

One week. It just didn't feel like it was long enough.

Hugh's office made an interesting comment on the man who occupied it. Five bolts of various tartans were propped in the corner—from muted hunting plaids to the Royal Stewart tartan. A mound of folders and paperwork sat on his desk. And the man across from her was staring back at her.

"What?" Sophie asked. "Do I have meat pie on my chin?"

"Aye." He reached over and wiped away a bit of gravy from the corner of her mouth. The gesture was very intimate, but not as intimate as what he did next. He stared into her eyes for a long moment.

He broke the spell, looking away. "I have to get back to work. Can ye make it to the workshop on yere own?"

"Certainly."

"I'll leave the auto for ye for later." He tried to hand her the keys.

She waved him off. "I'll walk. 'Tis not that far."

"I'll be here until late," he said. "Don't wait up for me."

"But—"

The phone on the desk rang, and he reached for it. "I have to get this." He turned his back, and their companionable lunch was over.

Sophie grabbed her coat and left. When she got back to the workshop, it was locked. She peeked in the windows, but didn't see the stubborn Willoughby with his key on the other side. She wandered into the building next to the kiltmaker's. Inside, she found what could only be a small café. Three women and two men sat at a table having lunch. One of them was Magnus, Willoughby's brother.

"Excuse me," Sophie said. They'd stopped eating when she'd walked in. "Do you know where Willoughby might be?"

Magnus harrumphed. "Doing a dance with the devil, for all I care."

The oldest woman playfully smacked Magnus's arm. "Don't mind him. They're feuding again."

"Here, come sit with us," said the youngest of the three women. She was dark-haired and petite. She scooted over and made room for Sophie. "We can get Elspeth to ladle up a bowl for ye in the kitchen."

"No, thanks. I already ate." With the Laird.

The first woman made the introductions. "I'm Hazel, this is Taffy, and this is Lara, the babe of the group. This one is my husband, Harold, and of course, ye know Mr. Grumpy Pants here, one of the wool brothers. If ye're looking for Willoughby, he probably has gone home for a wee nap."

Magnus harrumphed again and muttered, "Lazy bum."

Taffy rubbed Magnus's arm this time. "Be kind, luv. He's much older than you, and he needs his nap to make it through the afternoon."

First, Sophie really didn't believe that Willoughby could be that much older than Magnus, maybe a year or two. Second, it looked like Taffy had a bit of a crush on the old weaver.

The young woman piped up. "How about I walk you back?"

Sophie had a feeling that Lara wanted to pump her for information about why she was here…and with the Laird. The woman seemed so nice that Sophie didn't mind. "Sure."

Lara wiped her mouth and grabbed her coat.

When they got outside and before Lara could get in the first question, Sophie asked her what she did for the wool mill—"I dye the wool"—and kept her talking until they reached the kiltmaker's workshop.

"This is me. Thanks for the company," Sophie said and ducked inside. Unfortunately, Willoughby hadn't taken a long nap and was back at his place, making a kilt out of the Royal Stewart tartan. Mrs. Bates was there, too, sewing on buckles. He gave Sophie a withering glare.

"Sorry, I'm late." It wouldn't be gracious to mention his nap. She got right back to work on the Laird's kilt.

At five o'clock, they cleaned up the shop and Willoughby locked up. It was dark out, but the light was on in Hugh's office as Sophie walked by. When would he make it home?

She began the trek to Kilheath Castle, walking a ways with Hazel, Harold, and Lara, her new acquaintances. By the time

Sophie made it to Hugh's home, she was very glad to see the Wallace and the Bruce. She expected to see Hugh's aunt, but Davinia wasn't in the house.

After taking the dogs for a walk, close to the house this time, Sophie heated up her dinner. She sat in front of her therapy lamp, eating her haggis stovies while the hounds rested at her feet. She felt good about the day, but something nagged at her…when was Hugh getting home?

She pulled out her phone, but Amy hadn't responded yet to her texts or her voice mails. Sophie sent messages to both Emma and Ramsay—whom she could trust to get it done.

When you see Amy, tell her to call me.

Sophie's eyes started to droop. She and the dogs hauled themselves upstairs. She looked in every bedroom, but found none had been furnished yet, which explained why Davinia hadn't moved in today.

Sophie had two choices: She could pass out in Hugh's bed or sleep in his sister's room. She decided to do both. For now, she and her dog friends would cuddle in the master's bed. Later, when Hugh got home—if he didn't come crawl into bed with her—she'd sleep beside him again on the floor.

She changed and snuggled under Hugh's quilt, feeling a little cheated—the Laird hadn't kissed her once today. Interesting how quickly she'd grown accustomed to his lips on hers.

Sophie woke up an hour later to a thump and a litany of swear words in a baritone hiss. Oops. Maybe she should've picked her things up off the floor before she went to bed. She expected the bed to dip down like the first night, and she lay there in glorious anticipation. But the bedroom door clicked shut, and she was alone.

In the room next to hers, the Laird was making up his pallet, still cussing on and off. When he grew quiet, Sophie stole out of bed and sneaked in to sleep next to his warm body with her arms wrapped around him.

— ꕥ —

Hugh laid his arm on top of Sophie's and held her hand, not sure why she insisted on torturing him like his. God, didn't she know he'd stayed away tonight on purpose? She was too tempting for him—a man half-dead inside. Fortunately, she cuddled his back, instead of slipping into his arms for him to spoon her—or else, Sophie Munro might've had quite a surprise pressing up against her bum.

It took everything in him not to turn and face her, kiss her, and to love her all night long. But he could last her time here and keep his lips off her. Couldn't he?

Sophie's breathing evened, and Hugh raised her hand to his mouth and kissed it. She sighed in her sleep and pressed her hips into him from behind.

God. She was going to be the end of him!

Hugh had done something for Sophie today. He'd made a call to his friend Liam, his roommate from university, an art dealer now. Liam agreed to overnight a vase that Hugh had admired in his friend's study on his last visit to Perth. Aye, it was impulsive, but Hugh hoped the gift would be a comfort to Sophie when she was gone from here.

For a long time, he lay in her embrace. When he'd gotten home, the first thing he'd done was check the four other bedrooms.

But the bedroom furniture hadn't been delivered today as promised. Hugh checked Aunt Davinia's room on the main level, and it was still empty, too. He was getting the stinking suspicion that someone had canceled his order at the furniture store in Inverness.

He shouldn't be surprised that Aunt Davinia had hacked into his home computer again. He'd have to confiscate her key to the castle!

He didn't understand why Davinia and Amy were so hell-bent on finding him a wife. His parents hadn't been particularly happy being married, though maybe he was only remembering the time after Chrissa's accident.

Sophie squeezed his hand in her sleep, and a memory came flooding back. The family had been sitting in their pew at church on a summer Sunday. For once, he and Chrissa were behaving while the pastor droned on. Hugh had looked up to see his parents share a look—a look of love and connection. He'd watched as his da had taken his mum's hand, and she'd squeezed it back.

And Hugh remembered how comforted he'd been, how happy.

Grief had a way of masking the nicer emotions, and he'd forgotten how his parents had really loved each other.

Hugh kissed Sophie's hand again. A warmth spread into his chest, and he felt lighter than he had. He closed his eyes and went to sleep, content.

—◦◦◦—

The next morning when Sophie awoke, she was alone, and the Laird was gone from the castle. He'd been thoughtful enough to leave her the car, but she walked to the mill instead, as the weather had turned unseasonably warm for the Highlands. She worked with Willoughby, ate lunch with her new friends in the café, and made headway on the kilt for Hugh. The only time she saw him was through his office window, when she was leaving the mill in the evening. He sat at his desk in front of the computer, his back to her.

At the castle, she ate alone except for the hounds, who looked longingly at her smoked haddock flan, left by Mrs. McNabb. While Sophie sat in front of her therapy lamp, she felt pretty sorry for herself. She missed Hugh…his lips and his companionship. When she trudged off to bed, though, she found a vase on Hugh's dresser with a note propped in front of it.

For Sophie:
Fiat Lux
(Let there be light)

"It's so beautiful!" she exclaimed to the Wallace and the Bruce. They weren't particularly impressed, barely raising their heads from where they rested on the master's bed.

She carefully picked up the vase, running her hands over the smooth exterior. It was all luminous blues and greens that seemed to shimmer with an internal light source, which reminded her of a loch with a sun at the bottom.

"I can't believe he did this." But Sophie had known for a long time what a good heart Hugh had. Amy had told her what had happened when her parents had died. Hugh had sat quietly with Amy after the funeral, knowing she simply needed him there, not to talk, but to understand.

Sophie replaced the vase and readied for bed. When she climbed under the covers, she gave one last glance at her gift from Hugh before turning out the light.

Much later, when she heard Hugh in the room next to hers—and was sure he was asleep for the night—she crawled in next to him. She wrapped her arm around his waist and pressed her lips to his back.

"Thank you," she whispered.

He didn't wake up. She cuddled close and fell asleep.

The next three days passed pretty much the same, except there were no surprises waiting for Sophie on Hugh's dresser. She longed for time with the Laird, but it felt like she really was spending the week alone. Apparently, Hugh had gone on a hunger strike, disdaining to eat lunch with her again. Or dinner. Her time at the wool mill had turned precious, as she had grown very fond of the other workers she'd met. Willoughby had softened toward her, too, and Magnus was nothing but a big marshmallow under his crusty exterior.

Friday arrived, Sophie's last day. She would miss them all terribly when she went home tomorrow. Across the table from Willoughby, she picked up her scissors and trimmed the threads on the Laird's kilt, thinking about her quiet evenings at the castle.

Aunt Davinia must've left the country, because Sophie hadn't seen or heard a word from her. Amy still wasn't taking her calls or answering her texts. When bedtime rolled around at Kilheath Castle, Sophie would stretch out in Hugh's king-sized size bed with her two four-legged friends. Her hearing had become as acute as the hounds'. For when Hugh slipped into his sister's room late every night, Sophie would go sleep with him.

She'd started out sleeping with him to give him comfort, but cuddling him had become a comfort for her, too. Now she yearned for more. She loved cuddling up against him, but she was starting to feel rejected...though, to be fair, he always rested his arm over hers and held her hand in his sleep.

He hadn't kissed her since Sunday, and he hadn't laid a hand on her consciously—either above her sweater or underneath it. She was losing her one chance to make love to Hugh McGillivray, a chance of a lifetime, but she had a plan for tonight.

Tonight, she'd be more brazen. It was no longer about losing her virginity, or being properly shagged before she left tomorrow evening. She truly cared for the Laird.

"Lass?" Willoughby barked at her. "Did ye not hear me? Damned daydreaming again. What's got into ye this afternoon?"

"Nothing," Sophie said, smiling at the old fellow. "I'll miss ye, is all."

"Well, grab that buckle over there and get to sewing it in place."

"I thought Mrs. Bates sews all the buckles on. You said that she was the only one beside yereself that you trust to do it right." Sophie held a swatch of tartan over her heart. She'd found a place in this old man's shop, and she'd grown comfortable enough to goad him a little.

"Don't be cheeky with me," he rattled. "It would serve the

Laird right to have his kilt fall off because of an ill-placed buckle. The man never should've stuck me with ye. Now get to sewing."

Sophie put down the scissors and hugged the old dear. "Ye'll miss me, too, won't ye?" She kissed his cheek.

The poor man was so stunned that he froze for a good ten seconds. He finally sighed, and his shoulders sagged. "It will be quieter here without ye. Do you need help with where to place the damned buckle?"

"Aye. That would be grand." Though Sophie had seen Mrs. Bates put enough buckles on to not need further direction.

Willoughby spent the next five minutes instructing her on proper buckle placement and another five telling her the importance of using good strong thread and small stitches for this part of the process.

At five o'clock, he brought out tissue paper and a box for the Laird's completed kilt.

"Take it on up to the big house and show the Laird what ye've made."

She doubted Hugh would be home for dinner again tonight. She thanked Willoughby for everything and hugged him one last time before he locked up the workshop.

"Good luck to ye, lass." He patted her on the shoulder awkwardly. "Ye're a fine seamstress, and ye'll make some man very happy someday when ye get married."

Sophie adjusted Willoughby's scarf and then walked away, holding the box with the Laird's kilt inside. She couldn't concern herself with marriage any longer, but she intended to make one man very happy tonight.

---

Hugh was well aware that Sophie was going home tomorrow. Part of him couldn't wait to get his life back to normal—where he could concentrate on something more than the lovely body that snuggled up to him every night—and another part of him wanted to roar at the thought of her leaving.

Every night with Sophie's arms around him, more and more memories had come back—showering his consciousness, bathing him with goodness. Happy memories. Memories of his family and how they'd loved each other.

He hadn't slept on Chrissa's floor only after her death. He'd slept there every Christmas Eve from the time she was a baby, reading her 'Twas the Night Before Christmas before she went to sleep.

He remembered the times he'd spent at the wool mill while learning the operation from his parents, knowing they were proud of him.

And he remembered their family meals. He'd forgotten how happy they'd all been together, and now, somehow with Sophie cuddled up against him, he could remember the good and forget the bad.

Hugh turned out the light in his office, locked up, and left, thinking to surprise Sophie by being home for dinner. He'd called Mrs. McNabb earlier and asked her to leave them a dinner including haggis potato apple tarts. His cook had gone silent for a second, but she didn't question his choice. It was his favorite, and he hadn't asked for it since his sister's death.

All his staff and the whole town knew he had a houseguest, and he was sure the grapevine had been speculating...one of the reasons he'd put in long hours this week. Aunt Davinia had left him a note.

Urgent business in London and apologies for leaving poor Sophie to the gossip.

I'm sure you can make it right by the lass, and do something to salvage her reputation.

Auntie was as subtle as a bulldozer.

He rushed home, looking forward to surprising Sophie with a nice dinner. He wasn't trying to make it romantic, but he did have Mrs. McNabb set the grand dining room table for them. He hoped she'd found the candlesticks that had been packed away long ago. He walked a little faster.

As he rounded the last bend, something caught his attention out of the corner of his eye. The outside light was on, and part of the loch was illuminated. Hugh heard Sophie's voice, speaking quietly, calmly, before he actually saw her.

"It's okay, boy, I'm coming out to get ye. Stay calm." Sophie's arms were in front of her, and she was shuffling her way out to the center of the loch.

"Holy fuck!" he whispered. His mouth went dry. One of his hounds had fallen through the ice, and she was going out to get him. That's when the Bruce, standing at the shore, saw him and began barking. Hugh took off running.

"Sophie," he yelled. "Don't move." I'm coming.

She glanced up, but didn't acknowledge his warning. She kept talking to the Wallace as she crouched down to lie on the ice.

Good girl. She knew to distribute her weight.

He was close, so close. But as she inched toward the struggling Wallace, he heard the ice cracking, a sound so familiar that it jarred his bones. The sound of death.

He couldn't get there in time. Just as she reached for the Wallace, the ice crumbled, and she went in, too.

Oh my God, not again! He ran to the edge of the loch, but stopped short. He wouldn't make the same mistake twice. "Hold on, Sophie," he said gruffly. God, he hated leaving her. But he ran full-out for the ghillie's shed and the rope hanging inside. He grabbed Chrissa's sled off the wall, too.

Back outside, he saw she had the Wallace in a death grip in one arm and struggled to tread water with the other. As he rushed back to the ice, he tied the rope to the sled.

"Are ye okay?" He read somewhere that talking to the victim could help keep them calm. "I'm on my way."

"Hurry," she said breathlessly.

He slid the sled out to her. "I need ye to grab on to this." He hoped her hands weren't too frozen.

"I'll try." When it reached her, she got a hold of it, but it slipped from her hand.

"Again, Sophie." He couldn't lose her.

"I don't know if I can."

"Ye'll do it for me. For the Wallace. And for the Bruce." The damned dog was still barking encouragement from the shore. "Grab on to it because we need ye, lass."

She seemed energized by his words. This time when she grabbed the sled, she held on, gritting her chattering teeth. "P-pull, dammit," she growled.

Hugh pulled the rope. The weight of the wet dog, Sophie, and her wet clothes was more than he'd expected. The Bruce barked more.

"Help, ye stupid mutt."

The Bruce ran for the end of the rope, gripped it in his teeth, and tugged. Sophie and the Wallace came out of the water.

"Ye're a damned good dog," Hugh grunted as he pulled. They weren't out of danger yet. It took everything in him not to run out and help her the rest of the way, but he kept tugging until at last he had her.

"I'm cold," she said through chattering teeth.

He picked her up and rushed for the house.

"What about the W-Wallace?" she whispered.

He glanced back. "He's coming. The Bruce is nudging him along."

Hugh took her into the house, the dogs following, and straight up to his room. He flipped the switch on the gas fireplace to warm the interior and headed to the en suite bathroom. He turned on the towel warmer with one hand before stepping into the Roman shower, fully clothed with Sophie still in his arms. He turned on the water, letting the spray wash over them.

"We don't want the water too hot," he explained calmly. His darling Sophie was shaking so. "I promise this'll raise your temperature." He carefully set her on the stone bench with water cascading over her. "I'm going to take yere wet things off so we can get the warm water to your skin."

"O-k-kay."

While he steadied her with his body, he pulled off her boots and socks. Then he undid her waterlogged coat and removed it.

"Ye know, lass, many times this past week," he said, trying to give her a playful smile, "I've imagined peeling yere clothes off of ye, though never under these circumstances."

She gave him a valiant smile, but shivered violently, sputtering when water got in her mouth. "I hope I don't drown first."

"Ye're my braw lass." He laughed, knowing it was a good sign that she was spouting off at him at a time like this. "Come on. Let's get this sweater off of you. Ye can leave on yere bra." He eased it over her head as her next sentence registered.

"I'm not wearing one." And she wasn't.

"Oh, God." He thought he might hyperventilate. "Ye're beautiful, lass."

"Ye're just hard up." Her teeth chattered, and her arms were plastered down at her sides.

He kissed her. He couldn't help himself—he was such a bastard to take advantage of her. But she kissed him back, melting into him as he held her tightly.

"Oh, Sophie, I don't know what I would've done—" He broke off.

She shh'ed him. "It's o-okay, Hugh. I'm okay."

Fortunately, the way he was holding her kept her from seeing his face. Raw emotions coursed through him—anger, relief, gratitude, and terror. Gradually, the warm water left only joy where cold and upset had been. They stayed like that for a long while, until she wasn't shaking nearly as much and he was feeling calmer.

Finally, he remembered his duty. "Let's get these pants off

of ye, too."

"You f-first." A bit of laughter was in her voice.

"Oh, God, don't tell me that ye're not wearing any skivvies." He looked down, which was a huge mistake. Her wee perfect breasts were right there in his line of sight, and he was as hard as a rock.

"I'm wearing skivvies, as ye say. It's just that, ye know, they're a wee bit slutty." Her cheeks were pinking up nicely, a good sign she was going to be fine.

He brushed her cheek. "Well, close yere eyes, lass, so ye won't see me when I'm scandalized by yere underthings."

He didn't wait for her consent but undid her pants and pushed them down to her ankles.

"Step out." His voice was hoarse with his face inches away from the black lace of nothing that she wore. And God help him, he put his mouth over the small V and gave it a worshiping kiss. Before he did more, he rose. "How are ye feeling?"

"Do that again, and I'd be damned near on fire."

"Let's get you dried off and warmed up under the quilts." Keeping his boxers on, Hugh stripped out of his soaked shirt and pants, leaving them and Sophie in the running water while he toweled off. He dressed in fleece pants before grabbing two warm towels from the rack.

He turned off the shower, swaddled Sophie in the towels, and carried her to his room. For once, the Wallace and the Bruce weren't on the bed, but were in front of the fireplace. The Bruce was lying up against the Wallace, licking his ear.

Hugh pulled back the covers with one hand while he set Sophie down. "Slip off those panties so yere bed won't get wet." He wanted to do it himself, but was pretty certain he wouldn't be honorable in what he did next.

"My bed?" She looked at him incredulously. "Where are ye going?"

"Don't worry, lass," he chuckled. "I'll be right back." He went to the en suite and grabbed the other warmed towels and wrapped them around the Wallace.

He hurried back to the bed and pulled her into his arms, knowing the skin-to-skin contact was a good way to keep her warm. He tried not to think about her being naked, but she kept nibbling at his neck.

He looked up at the ceiling at the crack that had formed the year Chrissa died. It was past time to fix it. "I want to thank you."

She stopped in mid-nibble. "For what?"

"For lying next to me these last several nights." For helping him to remember his family in a good light.

She pulled away. "So ye were awake?" Her words were filled with hurt and disbelief. "The whole time?"

"Aye."

She sat up, scooting away from him. "Ye pretended to be asleep, because what? I was too plain to have in yere bed?"

He pulled her back into his arms and kissed the top of her head. "Calm yereself, woman."

"I'm going home tomorrow," she whispered angrily. "I don't want to go home a virgin."

"Nay. Ye're staying here with me. I mean to make you my wife." He'd made the decision subconsciously while she'd held him night after night. He couldn't ever let her go.

The word virgin finally sank into Hugh's brain. "Ye're a what?"

# CHAPTER SIX

"Ye mean to make me yere wife?" Sophie's voice was shrill. Water must still be in her ears. Or the chill had screwed with her brain.

"I'm finally going to do as Amy and Aunt Davinia bid me to do." He looked confused—like he was saying one thing while puzzling over another. "They've nagged me to marry you for the last year, and now I will."

An arrow pierced straight through Sophie's heart. Not one of Cupid's arrows either.

Something was very wrong with how she was feeling. She had liked Hugh even before she'd met him. Amy's stories about Hugh and their misadventures as children and young adults had painted him in the most lovable light. When Sophie had seen him for the first time, she'd contracted a serious case of lust over him, though he'd been a prat.

Then somewhere along the line in the last week, she'd fallen hopelessly in love with Hugh McGillivray, the flesh-and-blood man. The real deal. Perhaps it had happened when they were isolated at the cabin and he'd shared his deepest, darkest secret with her so she would know she wasn't alone in her pain. Or maybe while she'd been holding him night after night while he lay next to his dead sister's bed. Hell, as hard up as she was, she'd probably fallen in love with him on the first night… when she'd seen him naked.

Shouldn't she feel grateful to him that he'd given in to his relations' hounding and had agreed to marry the unmarriageable Sophie?

Except she couldn't marry him if he felt forced into it!

"Get me some pajamas," she said coolly, pushing away from him. "I need my cell phone, too." Being demanding was better than crying.

"Ye don't need pajamas." His voice was as hard as the ice on the loch should have been.

"I do. And don't forget the phone." She was going home—now. She wasn't going to inflict herself on him any longer.

Hugh had a confused expression on his face as he rolled out of bed. He pulled his pajama top from the closet and retrieved her cell from the dresser. She wouldn't look at the beautiful vase he'd given her. She wouldn't.

"Here." He left her with the things and went into the loo.

Sophie couldn't tell him the truth. It was too painful. If only he wanted her for the right reasons!

She would not crumple into a heap. Not now. She started to call Mama, but no way did Sophie want to be stuck in a car with Mama questioning her all the way back to Gandiegow. Sophie pulled on Hugh's pajama top and dialed the one person who wouldn't badger her to death about what had happened and how she was feeling.

"Ramsay, it's me, Sophie. I need ye to come and get me," she said, starting to shake, and not from the cold either.

"Give me the address," Ramsay said. "I'll leave now."

She gave him the directions and hung up. She looked up and found Hugh standing in the doorway.

"What's this about?" he said roughly.

The dogs raised their heads and gave her a questioning stare. They all waited for her answer. She didn't have the energy to speak. It had been a harrowing evening, and the depression was swallowing her and taking her words with it.

"Ye're not going anywhere," he said.

Sophie didn't meet his eyes, but went to the dresser and scooped out her panties, laying them on the comforter. Hugh's eyes flashed with desire at her slutty undies, but then his glare went icy cold in the next second.

She went to the third drawer and pulled out a turtleneck, jeans, and a sweater. She opened her mouth to tell him to step out of the room while she dressed, but he'd already seen all she had—maybe even seen to her very soul. She had a moment of gumption as she pulled his pajama top over her head like she was a snake shedding its skin. A new woman. Naked, but with a new determination. She silently dared Hugh to say something as she put on a warm turtleneck.

He glared at her with his hands on his hips. "What has got into you?"

"Nothing's got into me." Amy and Aunt Davinia would have to come up with a new woman for Hugh to wed. And bed.

But underneath it all…Sophie was amazed that during Hugh's non-proposal—somewhere, somehow—she'd found her own worth.

She didn't have to marry to feel like a whole person.

He grabbed her arm. "Talk to me, dammit. Don't shut me out." He paused for a second as if the answer had occurred to him. He dropped her arm and stepped back. "Do ye need time in front of yere lamp?"

The question knocked the air out of her.

She grabbed a pillow and threw it at his head, wishing for more—like a club to use on his thick skull.

He'd done her a favor with his last words, reminding her that she was damaged, defective, giving her just enough energy to go. She jammed all her clothes into her suitcase. She looked mournfully at the vase. She couldn't keep it without thinking of him. She left the vase sitting on his dresser. As she wheeled her bag to exit, he stood in the doorway, blocking it.

"Don't," he said through clenched teeth.

But he was settling. He didn't want to marry her. Maybe he thought it was time he tied the knot. Ultimately, he wanted to get married only because his family wished him to. The Laird may not love her, but Sophie had finally figured out that she loved herself.

She pushed past him. "Come, boys, walk me downstairs." The Wallace and the Bruce followed her down the stairs, one towel staying on the Wallace until he hit the final step.

Sophie went into the parlor, wishing she could make a quick getaway, but Ramsay wouldn't arrive for some time. She threw a log on the fire for the hounds, and then sat at the writing desk to do some light therapy as she waited.

The longer she sat in front of her lamp, the sadder she felt. She was going home defeated and would live with her parents for the rest of her life. The truth was, she would miss being at Kilheath Castle, miss holding the Laird while he slept.

She loved Hugh—there was no denying it—she only wished he loved her back. She wiped away a tear. And just in time, too.

Hugh brought a tray in and set it down on the coffee table.

"Eat," he said. "Drink. Refuel." He didn't seem capable of full sentences.

Sophie turned off her lamp, unplugged it, and carefully wound up the cord. She put it with her other things by the parlor entrance before walking to the tray, all the fight gone from her. She grabbed a tart and the mug of tea.

He pointed to the loveseat. "Sit."

She couldn't relax as she had on her first day here, when she'd pretended to be queen of the castle. All those illusions had been vanquished. The dogs came to lie next to her as if they didn't want to miss one second of her being there either. As the time ticked away, Hugh seemed to inch closer to her, also.

After a long while, he sighed heavily as if the fight was all gone from him, too. "Ye have to tell me what happened. Ye owe me at least that before ye go."

A sharp rap sounded at the front door. For a second, Hugh kept staring at her like he hadn't heard.

The knock came again, longer and harder. Hugh stomped off toward the foyer.

What could Sophie say to the Laird? He hadn't asked for her hand. Even more glaringly, he'd said nothing of love.

Sharp voices from the hallway interrupted her regrets—having Ramsay fetch her had been exceedingly stupid. She certainly didn't want punches thrown in her name. Ramsay was her friend, and nothing else.

She grabbed her luggage as she hurried from the parlor. The dogs popped up and followed. She found Hugh in the foyer, standing nose-to-nose with Ramsay.

"What's this?" Hugh said to her accusingly.

"He's my ride."

—◈—

Hugh wanted to punch the bloke in the jaw. He remembered him—Ramsay, Amy had called him. He was from Gandiegow, the same huge fellow Sophie had left with from the céilidh last summer. Where Hugh had acted the stubborn prat. He should've danced with Sophie. He should've made her his then.

He stepped into Sophie's path. "Ye don't have to do this, lass."

The Wallace and the Bruce each rubbed up against her, also presenting their arguments as to why she shouldn't leave.

Ramsay looked to Sophie. "What is it? Stay or go?"

"I'm ready." She sounded sad, but determined.

The bloke grabbed her bag and her lamp. For a moment, Hugh thought Ramsay might give them a moment to say good-bye in private, but the bastard just stood there, waiting for Sophie to go out first.

Hugh reached for her, but she sidestepped him and fled into the night.

Ramsay shrugged. "The lass has made her decision." And he was gone, too, closing the door behind them.

Hugh punched the wall, barely feeling the bruising of his knuckles. The dogs whined. The Wallace went to the door and scratched at the ancient entry, barking. The Bruce began to howl.

"Enough," Hugh yelled, but it did no good.

"What's all this racket?" Aunt Davinia said, coming in from the kitchen. "I stopped by to borrow some clotted cream for tomorrow morning's scone and find this. Where's Sophie?"

The dogs ran to his aunt as if to tattle.

She glared at him sideways. "What did ye do, Hugh-boy?"

He ran a hand through his hair. "I didn't do anything. I told Sophie she was going to be my wife, and she couldn't be rid of me fast enough."

He didn't add that she'd left with another man. Not just any man. Ramsay and Sophie had a past. His Sophie! Hugh wanted to howl like the dogs.

Auntie snapped her fingers, and both beasts sat, as if turned to porcelain. She narrowed her gaze on Hugh. "So did ye tell the lass that ye've finally come to yere senses, that ye love her?"

"She didn't exactly give me the chance."

"No, ye didn't give her a chance," his aunt said. "She needed to hear it from you, how ye feel about her, the words from yere heart. What did ye do? Did ye just tell her how it was going to be? Of course that's what ye did!"

She motioned to the Wallace and the Bruce. "Dammit, Hugh, she's not one of the hounds. She wants to be asked. She wants to be wooed. She wants to be cherished." Auntie shook her head with more disappointment than he'd ever seen from her. "Get off yere arse and go after her. Do it right now, for goodness' sake."

He started to argue. But, dammit, it didn't matter that Ramsay might be a towering, warrior of a Scot, Hugh's equal. Hugh had something greater going for him. He loved Sophie!

"Come on, Wallace. Ye, too, Bruce. We're going after the mistress of the castle."

Sophie cried silently in the darkness as Ramsay drove. As she'd expected, she didn't have to explain anything to him. Ramsay was a good friend, and she hoped someday he'd find himself a good woman.

Back in home in Gandiegow, though, Sophie couldn't dodge her mama's scrutiny. Annie hovered and clucked, made her a cup of tea, and sat with her on the couch. At Mama's insistence, Da came in and sat with them, too.

Sophie didn't tell them anything, though Annie had tried every trick in the book to get her to spill it.

"Ye talk to her, Russ. She needs to tell us what happened so we can help her." Annie patted her on the hand, and then glared at Sophie's da.

Da leaned forward, giving Sophie a look of understanding. "Ye don't have to tell us a thing. Ye only need to give me the nod, and I'll give Hugh McGillivray a visit he won't soon forget."

Sophie loved these people, but she was done being their troubled daughter. "Nay. It's not Hugh's fault. It's me."

"What do ye mean it's yere fault? Nighean, ye're perfect," Annie said.

Sophie considered hurling her mug at the hearth, but it was Mama's favorite. "You and I know I'm far from perfect."

Maybe it was time for some gut-wrenching honesty between her and her parents. "I heard you and Da speaking before I left to housesit at Hugh's."

Her mother looked at her, confused. "About what?"

Da grabbed a fishing magazine from the coffee table and

leaned back in his recliner.

Just as he was opening the pages, Sophie jumped in with both feet. "I heard you two agree that I was past my prime. Too old to find anyone. Too bossy."

Da dropped his magazine, straightening back up, his attention on her. "What are ye talking about, hen? I never..." His voice trailed off.

Mama stared at Da, very serious-like. "No."

The two of them burst out laughing, Annie clutching Sophie's da.

"I don't see anything funny here," Sophie said. This day had gone from bad to worse.

Mama calmed a little and patted Sophie's arm. "Ye got it all wrong. We were speaking of Deydie, not you."

"Da, what's Mama talking about?" Sophie asked.

Her father pulled out a wrinkled handkerchief and dabbed at his eyes. He shoved it back into his pocket. "Yere mama and the other ladies of Gandiegow think ol' Deydie and Abraham Clacher would make a fine couple. But, good grief, I don't see it. That woman is too old and crotchety, and Abraham is too salty of a fisherman, for those two"—he chuckled again—"for those two to get married."

"See, nighean, we weren't talking about ye after all. Ye just misheard."

Sophie didn't have time to process the revelation as someone started pounding on the door. She went to answer it. Ramsay stood there, but then the Wallace and the Bruce tore past him in a blur and jumped on her.

They would've knocked her over, too, if two strong arms hadn't caught her. It wasn't Ramsay who had her either, and it wasn't Ramsay who was scolding the deerhounds.

"Down, boys," Hugh said. Ramsay had been shoved to the side

Ramsay tipped an imaginary hat at Hugh. "My work here is done." Then Ramsay was gone.

Hugh shut the door behind him, still holding on to her, keeping the dogs at bay—sort of. Based on the way he was holding her, he wasn't letting go.

The laughter in the living room had come to a complete halt. Da rose and came to stand near Sophie. Hugh wrapped a protective arm around her—or was that a possessive arm?—and pulled her tightly against his side.

"Do I need to have a talk here with yere young man, daughter?" Da was an inch shorter than Hugh, but her da was giving him a glare that would've had a lesser man running for the door.

"I'd introduce myself, sir, but apparently ye already know who I am," Hugh said respectfully, but firmly. "May I speak with yere daughter alone?"

Da looked to Sophie, and she nodded.

"I'll leave ye be," her father said. "For now. But the second she's done with ye, ye better let her out of your grasp." He glared at the hand that gripped her shoulder.

"Sophie, we'll be in our room, if ye need us." Mama took Da's hand and led him away.

Sophie broke free and went to the couch. The dogs went with her, climbing up, each laying their heads in her lap.

"What do you want, Hugh? I heard all I needed to hear back at yere castle."

A strange thought hit Sophie. If she'd been wrong about her parents and what they thought of her, maybe she was wrong about Hugh, too. She scratched the Bruce behind the ears as he groaned.

She kept her gaze down as Hugh walked into the living room and sat in her da's recliner. She did a double take. He was wearing the kilt she'd made for him.

"There are things I failed to say." His voice was a hoarse whisper.

The emotion behind his words forced her to peek at him. He sat forward, making the old recliner creak and looked vulnerable. She wanted to go to him and put her arms around him, but she couldn't…not until she was certain why he'd chased her through the night and what he'd come to say.

He leaned closer. "I got the order all screwed up."

"That doesn't make any sense." And it wasn't what she wanted to hear.

He cleared his throat and swallowed. "I should've told ye how much ye've come to mean to me, Sophie Munro."

The Wallace yawned loudly and stretched further across her lap.

She wanted to say, And? Because her traitorous heart was impatient and hopeful that Hugh really did care for her.

He took her hand. "I should've told ye that I loved yere arms being wrapped around me night after night."

Da harrumphed loudly from the other room.

Hugh glanced in that direction, but soldiered on. "I'm not afraid of the dark anymore. I haven't had a nightmare all week. But most of all, ye helped me to remember all the wonderful things in life—past, present, and future. Ye've healed me." He kissed her palm. "I should've told ye that I love ye. Ye made me whole again, lass, and I'd be a fool not to claim ye as mine for always."

Mama's "ahhh" slipped from under their bedroom door.

Hugh got down on his knee and took Sophie's other hand from the Wallace. "Please say that ye'll marry me, Sophie."

"Down, boys," she commanded, and for a second, Hugh pulled back. "Not you. You stay."

She fell to her knees and wrapped her arms around him, hugging him. Mama and Da started to bicker in the other room. Sophie didn't get a chance to answer Hugh before Mama burst through her bedroom door, dragging Da behind her.

"So what did ye say?" Her mother stopped short at the sight of Sophie and Hugh kneeling on her living room floor, arms around each other. "Oh. Then ye've told the lad yes?"

Sophie got to her feet, pulling Hugh to his as well. Da,

blushing and looking uncomfortable, was tugging Mama's hand, trying to get her to go back to the bedroom with him. But Mama wasn't budging.

Da shot Sophie a look. "Answer the lad, daughter, so yere mother and me can be off to bed."

Sophie turned to Hugh and gazed into his lovely brown eyes.

"Aye, I'll marry ye. But on one condition."

Both of her parents gasped.

Sophie ignored them. "I'll marry ye as long as ye'll always kiss me as ye do now."

"Aye," Hugh vowed.

She pushed his hair away from his eyes—eyes that held love for her. "Ye've become my sunshine in the darkness. Did ye know that?"

"And ye've become mine as well."

Hugh kissed her then, and the world spun deliciously out of control, making her dizzy with joy. When she opened her eyes sometime later, she was settled on the couch, her parents were off to bed for the night, and the Wallace and the Bruce were asleep in front of the fire.

And the Laird? Well, he was right where she wanted him. He was in her arms, nibbling on her ear, making plans about their life to come, all in that voice of his that had her melting a hundred different ways.

"And ye'll always be mine, Sophie," he declared.

She smiled obediently. "Aye. I know. Because the Laird says so."

"Nay. Because ye've made me so happy. And I'm going to spend the rest of my life making ye the happiest woman alive."

And he did.

—◦◦◦—

If you want to know when my next book will be out, please sign up for my newsletter at http://eepurl.com/STeAX

I love to hear from readers! Please contact me at www. PatienceGriffin.com

# OTHER BOOKS BY PATIENCE:

### *TO SCOTLAND WITH LOVE*
**Welcome to the charming Scottish seaside town of Gandiegow—where two people have returned home for different reasons, but to find the same thing....**

Caitriona Macleod gave up her career as an investigative reporter for the role of perfect wife. But after her husband is found dead in his mistress's bed, a devastated Cait leaves Chicago for the birthplace she hasn't seen since she was a child. She's hoping to heal and to reconnect with her gran. The last thing she expects to find in Gandiegow is the Sexiest Man Alive! She just may have stumbled on the ticket to reigniting her career—if her heart doesn't get in the way.

Graham Buchanan is a movie star with many secrets. A Gandiegow native, he frequently hides out in his hometown between films. He also has a son he'll do anything to protect. But Cait Macleod is too damn appealing—even if she is a journalist.

Quilting with her gran and the other women of the village brings Cait a peace she hasn't known in years. But if she turns in the story about Graham, Gandiegow will never forgive her for betraying one of its own. Should she suffer the consequences to resurrect her career? Or listen to her battered and bruised heart and give love another chance?

### *MEET ME IN SCOTLAND*

**You can run from your problems, but you can't hide from love in the Scottish seaside town of Gandiegow....**

When a video of her calling *happily ever after* "a foolish fantasy" goes viral, marriage therapist Emma Castle is out of a job—and off to Scotland. The tiny town of Gandiegow is the perfect place to ride out the media storm and to catch up with her childhood friend Claire. But also in Gandiegow is the one man she hoped never to see again.

She's successfully avoided Gabriel MacGregor since Claire and Dominic's wedding, only to find he's now the village doctor—and just as tall, dark, and devilish as ever. Claire and Dominic's blissful marriage, however, is not what it used to be. Soon Emma and Gabriel find themselves taking sides even as the sparks begin to fly between them. Can Emma help her friends—or regain her career—as she struggles with her own happily ever after?

### *SOME LIKE IT SCOTTISH*
**In the delightful new Kilts and Quilts novel by the author of *To Scotland with Love* and *Meet Me in Scotland*, the Real Men of Scotland are waiting. And it's a match made in Gandiegow...**

Kit Woodhouse's matchmaking business is such a success, she's expanding to the Highlands of Scotland where the hot, prosperous, and kilted are anxious to connect. Now, looking to fill her stable with eligible bachelors, Kit's arrived in Gandiegow to recruit potential Real Men of Scotland. It's not until she meets her tour guide that she discovers just how real they can be.

With his sexy grin, jeans, and black wellies, Ramsay Armstrong is an unpolished hulk of a Scottish fisherman—and a skeptic when it comes to romance. Not exactly a man of "pairing attributes" when talking marriageable matches, but he does make Kit's heart beat a little faster. Maybe it's the scent of the sea in his hair. Maybe it's the challenge. Maybe it's the thrill of the unexpected. Then again, maybe it's love.

## ABOUT PATIENCE GRIFFIN

**PATIENCE GRIFFIN** grew up in a small town along the Mississippi River, living life in a close-knit community. She loves to quilt and has gained some recognition with her September 11th Story Quilt which has toured the country as the property of the Pentagon. With a master's degree in nuclear engineering, she's a nerdy girl to the core, but loves to read books which make her laugh. She lives in Texas with a hyper Sheltie, a Bishon-poo and a bulimic stray cat.

CPSIA information can be obtained at www.ICGtesting.com
Printed in the USA
LVOW12s1739170615

442816LV00005B/428/P